School Days
with the Millers

Miller Family Series

School Days
with the Millers

Mildred A. Martin

Illustrated by **Edith Burkholder**

Green Pastures Press

**Scripture Verses are taken from
the King James Version**

School Days with the Millers

Children's stories with moral values

Miller Family Series

Printed in the United States of America

ISBN 1-884377-01-7 Paperback

Contents

1

Laura's First Day
Psalm 56:3

It was the first day of a new school year! The Miller home buzzed with excitement like a hive of busy bees in spring, for this year all the children would be in school except Baby Beth.

Seventh-grader Peter tried to behave as if the first day of school were just the same as any other day, but his eagerness showed as he stuffed pencils and ring-binders into his bookbag. Timmy's bookbag had been packed and ready several weeks ago, and he was darting impatiently back and forth through the kitchen. "We don't want to be *late* on the first day!"

"You could do something to help me," Sharon told him calmly as she set bowls and spoons around the table. "Bring milk and juice from the refrigerator, and don't get so excited! Fourth grade is going to last a long, long time."

Laura was strangely quiet as she sat on the high stool by the sink, with Mama combing her hair. Today would be Laura's first day of first grade, and Laura was suddenly scared. Laura had been looking forward to this day for so long, but now that it was finally here . . .

"What are you thinking about, Laura? Mama asked softly, clasping a golden brown barrette into the hair behind her daughter's ear.

"I'll probably flunk!" Laura blurted out the words that were churning around in her mind.

"What?" gasped Peter, Timmy and Sharon, turning to stare at their sister. "What do you mean, Laura?" Mama wondered quietly.

"I'm sure I'll flunk," Laura repeated, hanging her head. "I don't want to go to school. I won't be able to do the work right, and I'll flunk the first year. I know I will!"

"Laura, you won't, either, flunk," Sharon scoffed. "You're smart enough to do first grade work. Why, you can even read some already."

"No, you don't need to worry about flunking first grade yet," Mama said cheerfully. "So far as we know, Laura, you have a good healthy mind. Your studies may be hard sometimes, but they won't be *too* hard. Just do your best, and all will be well! Even if you *would* "flunk" first grade, we would still love you just the same." And Mama's arm went around the six-year-old in a comforting squeeze.

Laura felt a little better, but her stomach

still fluttered nervously as the Millers ate breakfast and prepared to leave for school. *I'm glad that Mama and Dad are coming along for the first morning,* she thought as she brushed her teeth.

At the Millers' church school it was customary for whole families to come together on the first day. Mothers and fathers, grandparents and babies filled the auditorium benches behind their students, and Brother Ken rose to address the group.

"Welcome to Sunnyside Christian School!" he announced cheerfully, smiling at the assembled children and grown-ups. "We have a whole new year ahead, and today is the very first day! I'm excited about that. How many of you are excited, too?"

Dozens of enthusiastic hands waved high in the air. Timidly, Laura raised her hand just a little bit and then let it drop into her lap again.

Brother Ken looked around at the children, and went on speaking in a more serious tone. "I won't ask you to raise your hands this time, but how many of you are also feeling nervous, scared or worried about your new school year? If you are, I'd like to tell you about *my* first day of school when I was a little boy."

Laura's eyes opened wide. Brother Ken was a big man! Could he have ever been a scared first-grader? She listened as he went on.

"When I was a first-grader, I walked to school

alone. We had just moved to a new community, but my parents had shown me the way to my school, and it wasn't far. I set off happily the first morning, swinging my lunch box in my hand. All I had to do was walk half a mile down a country road and turn a corner, then I would see the school. Everything went well until I was almost at the corner.

"Suddenly my feet stopped moving, as my eyes noticed something in one of the fields ahead. *One, two, three. . . twelve, thirteen, fourteen. . .* there were more cattle in that field than I could count, and I was sure some of them were bulls! Worst of all, it didn't look like there was any fence around the field, and I would have to walk right past it to get to my school! *What if one of those big bulls comes after me?* I thought fearfully. *I can't do it! I can't go past that field!*

"For several long , agonized moments I stood still, staring at the field ahead. What could I do? I didn't want to go crying home to my mother and ask her to take me to school. But what if some of those big cattle chased me . . . and killed me? Why did the farmer leave cattle loose in a field with no fence?

"I could only think of one thing to do: pray for God to keep me safe. My parents always prayed about things, so now I followed their example. 'Dear God,' I whispered, 'Please don't let those cattle chase me. Help me be brave enough to walk past that field and get to school, and please don't let the cattle get me!'"

"What time I am afraid I will trust in Thee. A Bible verse flashed into my mind. I had learned that verse in Sunday school, and now seemed like the perfect time to practice it. 'What time I am afraid I will trust in Thee!'

I opened my eyes and took one step forward . . . and another step, and another. *God will keep me safe,* I thought boldly. *He can stop those bulls, just like He stopped Daniel's lions!* Closer and closer my feet carried me to that scary field.

"The cattle noticed me coming, and some of them began ambling slowly closer to the road. Whew, they looked big! and one of them had horns, but . . . suddenly I burst out laughing. Now that I came close to the field, I could see something I hadn't been able to see at first. There *was* a fence around the field after all! The thin shiny wire of the electric fence had been invisible from a distance, but I could see it now. The cattle weren't loose, and they couldn't get me.

"Yah, Yah! Moo-oo, you old cows!" I yelled gaily, bubbling over with relief. Oh, I was *so* glad I hadn't given up and gone crying home to my mother! The day seemed extra bright and beautiful now as I ran happily toward my school."

Brother Ken paused, and his eyes seemed to look straight into Laura's. "My dangerous, scary field of cattle turned out to be nothing

11

dangerous after all," he said softly. "So, children, if you are feeling scared or worried about this school year, don't give up! Pray about your fear, and keep going. Trust in the Lord. Probably you will find out, just like I did, that there is really nothing to be afraid of."

Nothing to be afraid of . . . Laura's mind echoed. *Maybe I really won't flunk! Maybe it will be a good year.* She smiled and straightened her shoulders.

2

Faithful In The Least
Luke 16:10

The history test was over! Sharon turned her test papers upside down on her desk, and breathed a great sigh of relief.

I'm still not sure if I got everything right, Sharon thought as she put away her pencil. *I did my best. . . I studied and studied! This year I want to make straight A's in history.*

Sharon's first world history test this year had included a lot of important terms to define. *I remembered most of them, but what about those different kinds of writing?* Sharon worried. After all the test papers had been collected by the teacher, she opened her desk and took out her world history textbook.

"*Cuneiform,* and *hieroglyphics,*" Sharon muttered under her breath. Now, which was which? Paging through the first couple of chapters,

Sharon soon found the place she wanted. *So cuneiform was the Mesopotamian system of writing, and* hieroglyphics *were Egyptian,* she discovered. *Well I guess I got those two answers wrong on the test, 'cause I thought they were the other way around!*

Sadly, Sharon closed her book and returned it to her desk. A shadow of disappointment hung over her the rest of the day, whenever Sharon remembered her history test and those two wrong answers.

But a surprise awaited Sharon the next morning! Brother Ken asked a student to pass out the papers from the day before, and Sharon's history test soon landed on her desk.

"One hundred percent! Very Good!" The red-penned words caught Sharon's eye from the top of her test paper. "A hundred?" Sharon gasped, and looked again. Yes, that was her grade, in Brother Ken's familiar handwriting! Flipping open the stapled sheets of paper, Sharon looked for check marks but found none. A wave of happiness swept through Sharon, but was quickly followed by doubt. What about those two kinds of ancient writing she hadn't defined properly?

Sharon turned to the second page of the test and examined it closely. Yes, there it was: *hieroglyphics,* right after *Hammurabi's Code.* And no, she hadn't given the right answer! She had mixed up *hieroglyphics* with *cuneiform,* just as she had feared.

Confusion churned inside of Sharon as she stared unseeingly at the papers on her desk. *Brother Ken gave you 100%, so just accept it.* One voice seemed to be telling her. *He's the teacher, and so what if he made a mistake? You* know *the right answer anyway!*

But the other voice of her conscience spoke differently. "You can't keep that 100%, it wouldn't be honest," said a still small voice. "Go tell Brother Ken what happened, and then you will know you have done what is right. Being honest is much more important than getting a good history grade!"

And so at recess time when her classmates had gone out to play, Sharon hurried up to her teacher's desk with the test paper.

"Brother Ken, I'm afraid I didn't deserve to get a perfect score on this test," she told him sadly. See these answers?" and she showed him the two that were wrong.

The teacher stared at Sharon's paper in surprise. "Well, I must have made a mistake with my checking last night," he said soberly. You are right: these two answers are wrong. How did you happen to discover the mistake?"

Sharon explained quickly, and Brother Ken was silent for a moment. Then raised his eyes from the desktop and smiled at his pupil. "Sharon, I am very pleased that you came and told me this," he told her. "You did the right thing. Being honest is so important, and you were honest even though it would mean losing your perfect test grade. That shows you are a person who can be trusted.

"Your action today helped me make an important decision," the teacher went on. "Sister Margie, our first and second-grade teacher, has a large class this year. The school board has decided to give her some help, and they asked me whether I could choose a good capable girl among my oldest students, to be a teachers' aide."

Brother Ken paused and looked searchingly at Sharon. "We need someone who will enjoy working with the little children," he said, "and also someone who can be trusted with responsibility. Sharon, you have showed that you are honest and conscientious. The Bible says, "He that is faithful in that which is least, is faithful also in much." If you are honest and careful in little things, you can also be trusted with bigger responsibilities! What do you think, Sharon? Would you like to spend some time this year helping Sister Margie?"

Sharon's eyes shone. "Oh, I'd love to, Brother Ken!" she exclaimed. "What kind of things would I do?"

Brother Ken smiled back. "There would be a number of things you could do to help," he told her. You could have flashcard drills and other practice times for one group of children, while Sister Margie is teaching others. And you could give individual help to children who need extra

17

attention. And I'm sure you could do a good job of checking papers, since you have such a good eye for mistakes!" he laughed, and Sharon joined in.

As she made her way out to the playground that morning, Sharon's feet seemed to be floating several inches above the ground. For as long as she could remember, Sharon had dreamed of becoming a teacher someday; a teacher of little children. Were her dreams already coming true?

I'm so glad I was faithful in that which was least, Sharon thought. A picture of that history test came to her mind, with the grade changed from 100% to 96%, but Sharon only smiled. *It pays to be honest,* she mused. *I'm glad I was faithful in that which was least, and I want to be faithful also in much!*

3

Nothing But Goat Feed
Colossians 3:15

"What's in our lunches today?" Peter wondered.

It was the third Monday in September, and Peter was already starting to get tired of lunchbox food. "I hope there's something *good* today," he growled.

"Take a look and see for yourself," Sharon invited cheerfully as she fastened a little twist-tie on the last baggie of small red cherry tomatoes.

"Ugh, are you giving us cherry tomatoes in our *lunches*?" Peter sounded horrified. "Nobody else eats cherry tomatoes in their school-lunch!"

"You *like* cherry tomatoes, don't you, Peter?" Sharon said patiently.

"Yes, but we've been eating them all summer already," Peter whined. "What else are we going to have? Oh, no! Leftover popcorn, too! You know I don't like popcorn after it gets cold! Why can't you pack us something good?"

"I just pack what Mom tells me to," said Sharon. "And you *do* have a good lunch: a sandwich, cookies, popcorn, and cherry tomatoes. You ought to be thankful."

"*What* are we having in our lunches?" Timmy inquired, coming through the kitchen door.

"Nothing but goat feed!" Peter replied disgustedly before Sharon could say a word. "She's only giving us leftover popcorn and cherry tomatoes. Goat feed!"

Dad Miller was right behind Timmy, and his eyebrows drew together in a frown at his older son's words. "Peter! You may not talk that way about your food!" he rebuked sharply.

Striding across the kitchen, Dad looked down into Peter's lunchbox. Then he reached in and took out the sandwich and the nice little bag of homemade cookies. "Peter, you were not only complaining; you were also not telling the truth," Dad said, turning to face his son. "You said you had *only* popcorn and cherry tomatoes in your lunch, so that is what you will have today."

"But, Dad! Only that? I'll get so hungry," Peter moaned.

"This is a lesson you need to learn, Peter," his father told him. "We are very fortunate people, to have all we need to eat. Many of the people in our world today would think popcorn

and cherry tomatoes were a good *big* lunch. Along with a sandwich and cookies, that would be more than millions of people have to eat in a whole day! God has blessed our country with plenty, and if we are not thankful for it, we don't deserve it.

"God sees the misery of many starving people every day, and it grieves him. How much more it must grieve him if we, who have so much, are not thankful!"

Peter hung his head. "I'm sorry," he whispered.

Dad put his hands on Peter's shoulders. "If you have only popcorn and cherry tomatoes for lunch today, you should be hungry enough to appreciate them," he said. "And then in the future, it will help you to be more thankful for the good lunches you usually get."

In school that morning, Brother Ken read from the third chapter of Colossians for devotions. ". . . And let the peace of God rule in your hearts, to which also ye are called in one body; and be ye thankful . . ." he read aloud.

And be ye thankful! Peter's ears burned as he remembered his behavior earlier that morning. He thought about the meager lunch of popcorn and tomatoes awaiting him, and how hungry he might be by afternoon. He remembered his father's words about people in other countries who were starving. "I'm sorry, Lord," he prayed silently. "Help me to be more thankful, after this."

4

The Dreadful Paul
Romans 12:20

"Mama, why is there a song about The Dreadful Paul?" Laura looked up at her mother wonderingly.

"The Dreadful Paul?" Mama was puzzled. "Where did you hear a song like that?"

"You know, Mama, we sing it at school. 'See, He breaks the prison wall, throws aside the dreadful Paul'. . . that's what it says."

"She means *Mighty Army of the Young*, Mama!" big sister Sharon explained. Coming over to sit beside her mother and Laura, Sharon went on: "here's how it goes.

Mighty army of the young,
Lift your voice in cheerful song.
Send the welcome word along, Jesus lives!
See, He breaks the prison wall,

Throws aside the dreadful pall,
Conquers death at once for all, Jesus lives!

"Yes, I remember that song," Mama smiled. "You see, Laura, it isn't talking about a *person* named Paul. The word 'pall' means gloom or sadness. Jesus takes our sadness away."

"But Mama, there really is a dreadful Paul," Laura insisted. "He is in my class, but he's bigger than me, a second-grade boy. And he teases me all the time! Yesterday he put a dead animal's foot in my lunchbox, right beside my sandwich. And today he put a 'possum's tail in, and I thought it was a snake, and I just about screamed!"

"Where does he *get* stuff like that?" Sharon gasped.

"His big brother catches animals in traps," Laura explained. "So Paul had a 'possum tail and a foot from some other animal, and he put them in my lunch. He's mean! If he does anything like that tomorrow, I'm going to tell the teacher."

"I know a better idea," Sharon said wisely. "Why don't you put something *nice* in *his* lunchbox, Laura? Then he will be your friend, and be kind to you. What can she give Paul tomorrow, Mom?"

"We have those candy bars Grandpa gave us," Mama suggested. "That's a very good idea, Sharon. Laura, you may have an extra candy

bar tomorrow, and put it into Paul's lunch. That is the Christian way to treat those who are unkind to us. The Bible teaches that if we are kind to our enemies, the Lord will reward us."

The next day, when the children from Sister Margie's class opened their lunchboxes, Paul looked surprised. "Yippee! A candy bar. Who gave me this? My mom doesn't have any candy bars." He looked around questioningly at the other children.

Laura's face turned pink. "It was me," she admitted in a small voice. "I gave it to you."

Paul stared at her in confusion. "You funny girl," he mumbled. "Well, thanks!" His face was bright red as he opened the candy bar and took a bite.

"So, what happened to the 'dreadful Paul'?" Sharon asked her little sister at bedtime a few days later.

"Oh, it worked just like you said!" Laura replied happily. "Paul never teases me any more. And today he helped me with my art project when the teacher said the second graders could help the first grade. He's not a dreadful Paul now; he's my friend."

5

The Wrath of Man
Psalm 76

"Did you hear that we are going to have a special speaker for chapel this morning?" Peter's friend Joshua whispered as the boys stood in line, waiting their turn to walk into the auditorium.

"Who is he?" Peter wondered. Usually one of the students' fathers came to school for devotions on Monday morning.

"His name is Stanley Fox, and he's a friend of my dad," Joshua replied. "He was a missionary in Haiti, and . . ." the two boys fell silent as they saw Brother Ken looking their way.

A few minutes later, the children of Sunnyside School looked up expectantly as the visiting speaker took his place at the front of the room. Brother Stanley looked around and smiled at the students and their teachers.

"Good morning, boys and girls," he began. "Most of you don't know who I am. But *who* I am is not so important as *what* I am, and I'll tell you what I am. I am a soldier of Jesus Christ!"

Peter and his friends watched Brother Stanley intently. He was a fairly young man, younger than Dad Miller and not quite so tall.

"I would like to read a Psalm this morning," he went on, "about the power of God. Turn in your Bibles to Psalm 76." Brother Stanley began to read aloud in a firm, deep voice. The majestic words and phrases of the Psalm flowed through Peter's mind.

'In Judah is God known: his name is great in Israel ... he brake the arrows of the bow, the shield, and the sword, and the battle . . . Thou art more glorious and excellent than the mountains . . . The stouthearted are spoiled, they have slept their sleep: and none of the men of might have found their hands. At thy rebuke, O God of Jacob, both the chariot and horse are cast into a dead sleep. Thou, even thou, art to be feared: and who may stand in thy sight when once thou art angry? . . . the earth feared, and was still, when God arose to judgment, to save all the meek of the earth. Surely the wrath of man

shall praise thee: the remainder of
wrath shalt thou restrain.'

I wonder what that verse means? Peter
thought. *"The wrath of man shall praise thee . . ."*

Soon, though, Brother Stanley began talking about that very same verse! "Boys and girls,"
he said, "Verse ten of this Psalm reminds me of
something that happened during my years of
mission work in Haiti.

"When I was a boy, I often wondered what it
would be like to be a missionary in some faraway country. Well, when I was asked to go to
Haiti, I soon found out! Haiti is a country where
people openly worship the devil. Many sad and
scary things happen in Haiti. But the power of
God is always greater than the powers of evil,
and I have seen that fact proven many times.

"When I first moved with my family to be
pastor of a little church in the Santo Valley in
Haiti, we found the work difficult. That little
church just couldn't seem to get a good start.
Very few of the local people wanted to come. As
soon as I learned the language well enough to
understand what was going on, I found out what
the problem was. One of our neighbors, a man
who lived only 500 yards away, was a witch doctor! And not just a common, ordinary witch doctor either: this man was a voodoo bishop, an
important man in the worship of Satan. He was
a big, powerful man, six feet and three inches

tall, and everybody feared him. People didn't have much respect for the police in that part of Haiti, but they did respect and fear that witch doctor! Nobody dared to displease him.

"I watched this witch doctor at work several times when he held a public ceremony to try to heal a sick child. He would beat drums, and break glass bottles and cut himself and the child with the broken glass. He would dig holes and pour things into them, while he muttered weird incantations. Even if the sick people did not get well, the witch doctor still held tremendous power over the people's minds.

"I knew this man was our enemy, the enemy of the Lord's work. I started going over to his place to talk. I was polite and friendly, trying to win his confidence and show that I was not afraid of him. But whenever I would begin to speak of Jesus' blood and His death upon the cross, the witch doctor seemed to go crazy! He would shudder and shake, and order me to get out of his yard.

"Sir, I'd like to pray for you," I told him one day.

"'Don't you *dare* pray for me!' the witch doctor shouted, getting very upset.

"Whenever I talked with this man a crowd of Haitian people would gather and stand around watching to see what would happen. Now some of these people began to beg me to go home. 'Stay away from him! He will kill you!' they warned.

"But I stood my ground that day. I was not afraid; if I must die, I was willing to die for the sake of saving souls! The people around me didn't understand about the power of God, and it looked like an unequal contest: one skinny little white missionary against that huge, powerful priest of the devil. People were even hiding in the bushes to watch the big show!

"'Don't you dare pray for me,' the witch doctor shouted again.

"Yes," I repeated with determination. "I *will* pray for you."

"'Well, if you want to pray for me, *I'm* going to pray for *you* first,' he threatened. 'I'll make a deal with you! I will pray over you first. And if you are still here, alive and in one piece when I am finished, then you can pray for me all you want!'"

"I remembered the contest between Elijah and the prophets of Baal in the Bible. 'It's a bargain,' I replied boldly. 'You may pray first, and then I will pray!'

"Everyone watched fearfully as the witch doctor put his hand on my shoulders and began to read out of a small, dirty book. Then he began to pray in Creole, then in French, and then in other languages that I didn't know. The audience clearly expected me to fall down dead, or dry up and wither away! When nothing happened to me at all, I could hear the impatience in that witch doctor's voice. His babble of gibberish grew louder and faster. He drew lines and symbols on the ground, then almost knocked off my glasses as he made lines and symbols on my face with his finger. I didn't like that too well, but I knew that God's power is stronger than the forces of evil. I was praying in the Name of the Lord, even as he prayed to his evil spirits to destroy me, and the Name of Jesus was my protection. I could feel the devil around us, but the Lord was there with me too!

"When the witch doctor's ceremony finally ended, I was still there. Nothing had happened to me! I was not surprised, of course, but he was. All the watchers were silent, not daring to make a sound.

"Now it was my turn to pray! Grudgingly, the voodoo bishop knelt before me. Like little David facing the mighty Goliath, I came to him in the name of the Lord. In the Name of Jesus I prayed aloud for that evil man, that he would become sick of his sin, that he would want to repent and serve the Lord. I prayed harder than I had ever prayed in my life before, asking God to make him miserable until he turned from his wicked ways!

"Suddenly things started happening. I never saw the witch doctor stand up, but all at once he was on his feet and hitting me with his fists. '*Run!*' screamed all the watching people. 'Get back, Pastor Stanley!'

"Slowly I backed out of the yard, as the witch

doctor began throwing sticks and stones. 'Get out!' he hissed, shaking with anger. 'Get off my property, and don't you *ever* dare to come back!' and he began shouting terrible threats against me and my family.

"I went home, and that same week the witch doctor fell sick. Everyone went around talking about him in fearful whispers, for it looked like he was going to die. I shut myself in my bedroom and began to pray again for him: 'Lord, please spare his life! Let him have time to repent. What a powerful testimony that would be, if this wicked voodoo bishop became a Christian!'

"So the man recovered. But he was still angry. *'I couldn't make the spirits kill you, but I will do it myself!'* he threatened me. And he did try! Things were very tense in the village. Everyone knew that the witch doctor had become sick and gotten well again because I prayed. And everyone knew that he was after me! He bought a shiny new machete and dedicated it to the sole purpose of killing me. He boasted that he was going to cut my dead body into a thousand pieces and send them to witch doctors all over Haiti, to show what he could do to a preacher!

"Our friends in the village all begged me to stay away from that witch doctor, and to have nothing more to do with him. But one night just after darkness had fallen, the witch doctor himself came and knocked on my door.

"'Young missionary man,' he sneered, 'do you still say you aren't afraid to die?'

"That's right," I answered calmly.

"'I need a ride to town,' he said, eyeing me sharply. 'Will you take me in your pickup?'

"I could smell the liquor on his breath, and I knew he was dangerous. I thought about my wife and my little boys. But then I thought of Shadrach, Meshach, and Abednego in the Bible!

"Yes," I said politely. "I will take you to town."

"Hundreds of eyes were watching from their little huts as the witch doctor and I drove together down the winding streets of the village. All the people had seen the satchel in the witch doctor's hand, and they knew as well as I did what was in that satchel. The witch doctor and the missionary were driving away together in the dark, and the witch doctor had his brand-new machete with him! They must have wondered how the young missionary could be so foolish!"

A cold shiver ran down Peter's backbone. He and all the other students sat perfectly still, their eyes fixed on Brother Stanley. *What was going to happen next?*

"I *was* rather scared that evening," the missionary admitted, smiling. "But I knew that I was not alone in the truck with that witch doctor. I was praying steadily, and God was with me. After we had gone some distance down the road, my passenger reached for his satchel. He fumbled with the latches that held it shut, but the latches would not open! He tried again and again, muttering and swearing to himself, but he *could not* open that case!

"Relief and joy welled up inside me. God was protecting me again, just like He protected Daniel in the den of lions! God had shut that satchel with the machete of death inside, and my big, strong enemy was powerless to open it.

"There was a bewildered, defeated look on the witch doctor's face as he saw that he had failed again. Without a word to me, he rapped his knuckles on the truck door as the usual Haitian signal that he wanted to get out. I dropped him off at the street corner and drove home again, rejoicing and praising God all the way. There were watching eyes again at all the hut doors and windows, and I knew that soon the story would spread through the whole community! The witch doctor was beaten, and everyone knew it.

"The witch doctor himself knew he was beaten, too. When I walked past his house he still shouted at me, but his pride and arrogance were gone.

"'I prayed to the devil and all his angels to smite you and your family,' he told me angrily. 'But every morning I'd watch your house, and you all came out of that door as well and strong as ever! You gave me proof, and you proved to all the people of Santo Valley, that the power you serve is greater than mine!'

"And *I* say, hallelujah!" Brother Stanley went on. "That's exactly what I wanted. I trusted God to prove His power, and He did. He broke the evil power that this voodoo bishop held over the people of Santo Valley, and their fear of him was gone. After this happened, we had revival meetings, and the people finally dared to come! Many people gave their hearts to the Lord: both young people and old people. Even some witch doctors attended the services! The church began to grow in a mighty way.

"I believe that this is what the Psalmist meant when he said, 'Surely the wrath of man shall praise thee, and the remainder of wrath shalt thou restrain.' Even the wrath of that angry witch doctor turned out to be to the glory of God, as he admitted in his own angry words that God was more powerful. Man's wrath is restrained by God, too: the witch doctor was not able to hurt me. The Bible says, 'Greater is He that is in you, than he that is in the world.'"

6

The Field Trip
Psalms 104:24

"Mom! Our class is going to take a field trip next week!" Timmy's voice was shrill with excitement as he bounded into the kitchen.

"A field trip already? It's only October," Mama smiled at her excited son.

"Oh, we'll be taking another field trip at the end of the year, of course," Timmy explained. "But this time we are going to the Nature Realm Center, to see their natural museum and take a hike and eat our lunches there. And, Mom!" Timmy looked up at his mother pleadingly. "Couldn't you come along with us on this field trip? There are always some parents who go along, to drive and to help watch over us children. I wish you'd come this time!"

"Well, it sounds enjoyable," Mama answered slowly. "I would like to help chaperone one of your field trips, now that Baby Beth is getting bigger. Let's see what Dad says about it."

And so the following Tuesday Mama put little Beth into her backpack carrier and joined Timmy's class at school. Timmy, Philip, Frank, and Eugene were to ride with Mama in the Millers' station wagon, while the rest of the class had seats in two vans driven by other mothers.

It was a perfect day for a hike outdoors! Bright red and gold leaves adorned the trees along the highway, and sunlight streamed down from a nearly cloudless blue sky. "I saw a sign!" one of the boys cried out suddenly. "Nature Realm Center, five miles ahead!"

At last the vans and station wagon turned in at the nature center. Nineteen middle-grade students climbed out and stood looking around eagerly. "I see the museum building!" "Where are the hiking trails?" "My dad said there are stuffed birds and animals!" they chattered.

"Okay, boys and girls," Sister Joy took charge. "Let's all stay together in a group. We will tour the museum building first, and see some slides about the wildlife of our state. After the slides we will divide into four smaller groups to hike along the trails. Then we will meet back here and eat our lunch."

Bursting full of energy and excitement, the children followed their teacher toward the museum building under the trees. At least, some of them followed! Philip and Eugene dashed ahead of the group, shouting "I'll beat you there!" "No, I will!" Laughing and panting, they reached the museum doors first and turned to wait for the others.

"Boys, you must not run ahead like that," Sister Joy reprimanded when the group caught up. "Field trips are safer, and more fun, when everyone stays with the group. We want to keep together in the museum, too, so we can talk about the different exhibits we see."

The nature museum was full of wonderful things! To Timmy, who loved wildlife, this was the best museum he had ever seen. A long hall, full of lifelike trees, displayed all kinds of mounted birds and animals. There were skunks, raccoons, rabbits, and squirrels; crows, ducks, some ruffed grouse and an owl with shiny yellow eyes. A red fox appeared to be slinking behind a bush, and a family of deer stood proudly in the leaves.

"They all look like they are *alive*," whispered a girl to her friend.

"This sign says, *'Please Do Not Touch The Animals'*," Sister Joy read aloud. "Be sure you all obey the rule, Class, and leave these animals looking nice. Oh, look at the hawk!" she added, peering up at a large red-tailed bird that seemed to be swooping down upon her from the ceiling. The hawk's claws were extended, ready to pounce on its prey. "Eeeek!" A little girl screamed faintly, clutching at her teacher. "That looks so real! But I see the wires, so I know it isn't alive," she added with relief.

Soon the class came to a large window with double-thick glass overlooking a pretty little clearing in the woods. There were a large number of feeders filled with seeds and corn directly outside the window, and they were full of small wild creatures. "Shh!" Sister Joy cautioned. "If we are all still and quiet, we can enjoy watching them eat."

The class stood quietly gazing at the happy birds and animals. There were blue jays pecking at the sunflower seeds in a high tray, scattering them in all directions. One plump seed fell to the ground, and a striped chipmunk seized it. Another chipmunk chased him, and the two darted in and out among the feeders. A squirrel sat on his haunches nibbling at the grain of corn between his forepaws. "Look! a rabbit!" Timmy whispered excitedly, just as one of the girls cried softly, "Look, there are hummingbirds, at that feeder that looks like a big red flower."

When the watching children began to grow restless, Sister Joy led them on. "The wildlife slides will be over here, "she said, directing them to another room.

After they had seen the slides and the gift shop, the children emerged eagerly into the outdoors again.

"We have a little more than an hour before lunch," Sister Joy announced, "so now we are going to hike on the trails. We will divide into small groups. That way you will have a better opportunity to see more wildlife than you would with one big noisy group. Jennifer, Ruthie, Abigail, Mary, and Sarah, you may go with Abigail's mother. Timmy, Frank and Eugene. . ."

"I want to hike with *my* mom!" Timmy exclaimed.

"All right," Sister Joy smiled. "You three boys, and Philip and Jabez, may go with Mrs. Miller. We will meet back here in the picnic area at noon," she instructed when all the children were divided into groups. "Don't forget to take notes about the things you see!"

Timmy and his four friends frisked about like young squirrels themselves, as they moved off with Mama down one of the trails that led through the woods. "Boys, let's see how many kinds of trees you can identify in these woods," Mama suggested, stepping briskly along with baby Beth riding on her back. "This sign says these trees are *Black Oaks.* And those are *White Ash,* and I think I see a *Buckeye* farther on."

"*Why* do we have to write stuff down?" Philip complained. "It's such a bother!"

"Writing things down will help you remember more of the things you saw today," Mama told him. "Sister Joy is going to give you children a grade on the notes you take."

Rustle, rattle, crunch! went *something* through the dry leaves. "What was that?"

Eugene hissed, running toward the sound. "I'm gonna catch it!"

"No, boys, we must not try to catch any of the wildlife here," Mama said hastily. "This is a public park. We are not allowed to pick the flowers, or break any branches, or hurt any animals. We must leave the natural beauty unspoiled, for other people to enjoy."

"I don't know how to spell *Buckeye*," said Frank. Ripping the page from his little notebook, he crumpled it up into a wad. Drawing his arm back, he threw the paper wad with all his might! It bounced off a log and rolled down the hill, and disappeared into a ravine.

"Frank, you will need to go down there and pick that paper up," Mama said sternly. "Littering in a place like this is a serious offence!"

"Aww, do I really have to?" moaned Frank. "Nobody will ever be able to see it from the trail!" But seeing that Mama meant business, he headed down into the ravine and soon returned with the crumpled paper.

"Put it in your pocket until we get to a wastebasket," Mama told him kindly and walked on.

"I'm tired of going so slow," Philip murmured to Eugene. "Race you to that old stump!" and the two boys bounded down the trail.

"Write down *Hemlock*, and *White Pine*," Timmy called out, reading the signs before a stand of evergreen trees. "And what kind of birds are those?"

The little group wound its way through a patch of ferns, past a swamp full of croaking frogs, and under a tree which had a large gaping hole high up on the trunk. "I wonder who lives there," Jabez pointed. "Maybe a family of raccoons!"

Philip and Eugene kept hurrying ahead of the other four, not paying attention to the beauties around them. Instead of taking notes, they merely dashed back and forth along the trail.

Suddenly the hikers came to an open spot among the trees. "I can see the sky again," Timmy observed, blinking.

"What are those?" Jabez exclaimed. A clear, wild call sounded high in the sky: "coo-whook! "coo-whook!" and a V-shaped formation of birds came into view.

"Wild geese!" Frank shouted.

"Huh-uh, those aren't wild geese," Timmy disagreed, staring at the big birds. "They look like swans or something."

"Whistling swans!" cried Mama, shading her eyes to peer into the sky. "Look boys, do you all see them? That is a rare sight around here! Write it down in your notes: you saw a flock of whistling swans flying south for the winter. Beth, do you see the swans?"

"Birdie," the toddler replied, pointing at the swans with one plump little hand.

"Where are Eugene and Philip? They missed it!" Frank said ruefully when the flock of swans had passed from sight.

"Yes, I'm afraid they did," said Mama, looking down the trail. The two impatient boys had turned a corner, and were nowhere to be seen! "It's their fault, for running ahead."

A few minutes of walking brought the hikers to the end of their trail, at the picnic area. Some of the other groups had already arrived, and Sister Joy was looking at her watch.

"It's time for lunch, children," she called when everyone had gathered around the tables. "Did you enjoy your nature walk?"

"Yes!" "Oh, yes, we did!" "Thank you!" came a chorus of voices.

"Before we have prayer for our lunch, I want to teach you a Scripture verse," said the teacher. She quoted from memory:

"'O Lord, how manifold are thy works! In wisdom hast thou made them all: the earth is full of thy riches!' Psalm 104:24. I will say it again, and then I want you to repeat it with me."

"'O Lord, how manifold are thy works! In wisdom hast thou made them all: the earth is full of thy riches!'" recited the children.

While the group was eating their lunch, Sister Joy came over to sit beside Mama. "How was *your* hike?" She questioned with a smile. "Did your group behave, or did you have problems with some of them running too far ahead?"

"Yes, we did have some trouble with that," said Mama. Then she chuckled. "You know, when I was a schoolgirl, *I* was one of those children who were always running ahead of the group. So now I guess I'm just reaping what I sowed!" she remarked as the two women laughed together.

Mama? Timmy thought in disbelief. Could his own wise, grown-up mother have ever been a child like that? *I can't imagine,* he laughed to himself as he took a bite of his sandwich.

7

The Five-Dollar Glove
Psalm 15:4

"Hey, Andy! Where did you get that new glove?" Peter's eyes opened wide as he looked at the brand-new baseball glove on his friend's left hand.

"My aunt and uncle gave it to me for my birthday yesterday," Andy replied. Pulling off the glove, he showed it to Peter. "Isn't it something?" he gloated. "The very best kind! It would've been *way* too expensive, but they bought it at a discount store."

"And your old glove was still perfectly good," Peter observed, with a touch of envy. "What are you going to do with *two* ball gloves?"

"Well, would you like to buy my old one?" Andy offered, looking at Peter keenly. "It's real leather, and it *is* nearly new. I'll give it to you for five dollars, if you want."

"Sure!" Peter replied eagerly. "My old glove is so small, it's hard to get my hand into it anymore. I'd love to have yours! I'll bring the five dollars to school tomorrow."

At home that evening, Peter sought his father's permission. "Dad, may I buy Andy's extra ball glove for five dollars? He got a new one, and his old one is still really nice, and mine is too small. I'd use my own money," his words tumbled out in a rush.

"Whoa, Peter. Slow down," Dad grinned at his son. "Now, run that by me again, so I can get a better look."

Peter explained, more slowly this time. "Well, son, if the glove is still in good shape, I guess it would be a good idea," Dad answered. "Will this glove be good enough to last until you are through school?"

"I think so," Peter said confidently.

"Very well, then," Dad gave his consent, and Peter bounded away to get his wallet.

On the way to school the next morning, Peter reached into his pocket several times to make sure that his five-dollar bill was still there. As soon as he arrived at school, he went in search of Andy.

"Good morning! Here's your money," Peter said happily when he found his friend. "Do you have the glove?"

Andy avoided looking at Peter. "Aw, I sold it to Henry already," he answered, trying to sound casual. "He gave me *seven* dollars for it."

Peter couldn't believe what he was hearing. "But... but you promised it to me!" he protested. "I told you I'd bring the money today!"

Andy looked uncomfortable. "Henry paid me more than you would," he answered defensively. "I need the money. I already gave Henry the glove, so it's too late now."

Trying to hide his disappointment, Peter turned away. But a dark pall of gloom hung over his day. During recess time, it was hard to look at that nice leather glove on Henry's hand ... the glove that should have been his own!

"I'd like to see your new ball glove," Dad told Peter that evening, looking at his son with interest. "Did you bring it home?"

Peter gulped. "I didn't get it," he said huskily, looking at the floor.

"Why not? What happened?" his father wondered.

"It wasn't fair," Peter cried out. "Andy agreed to sell it to me for five dollars: and then he went and sold it to Henry, because he offered him two dollars more! Andy shouldn't have done that, should he?"

Dad looked sober. For a long moment he said nothing.

"No, Andy did not do the right thing," he replied at last. When we make business agreements, we should keep them. A man must always keep his word, even when breaking it would gain him an advantage. Remember the fifteenth Psalm, with that list of marks of a godly man?"

Dad Miller sat down on the couch and motioned for Peter to join him. Reaching for a Bible, he turned to the book of Psalms. "'Lord, who shall abide in thy tabernacle? who shall dwell in thy holy hill?'" Dad read aloud. "'. . . He that sweareth to his own hurt, and changeth not,' it says in verse four. When this verse says 'sweareth' it doesn't mean using bad language. It's talking about making a promise or agreement. The godly man 'changeth not', even though it turns out to be 'to his own hurt'."

Dad put his arm around Peter's shoulder. "You must forgive Andy, and not hold this against him," he said gently. "I am sorry that you had this disappointment, but let it be a lesson for you! I want you to be a boy who keeps his word, and a man who keeps his word. There will be times in life when *you* are tempted to break an agreement. When that happens, remember Psalm 15. . . and the five dollar ball glove!"

8

The "Backwards" Boy
Proverbs 17:5

"Mama, did you know we have a 'backwards' boy in my class?" Laura informed her mother one day as she ate her afternoon snack.

"*What* do you have, Laura?" her mother replied, puzzled. "Swallow your cookie, child, before you talk. You shouldn't speak with your mouth full!"

Laura swallowed. "Reuben is a backwards boy," she repeated clearly. "He does everything backwards, and he's in second grade! He's always putting his books upside down in class, and he starts writing on the back side of his notebook paper instead of the front. Sometimes he even has his shoes on the wrong feet. He writes things backwards, too."

"Yeah, I remember," Timmy spoke up.

"Reuben has *diss-lex-ia.* He had an awful time learning to read or write at all in first grade, last year. His parents had to take him to a specialist, to help his eyes learn to work right."

"What's dis-dis-lex-uh?" Laura wondered, looking worried. "Can other people catch it from him?"

"No, Laura," her mother reassured her. "Dyslexia is not contagious. Dyslexia is a learning disability, and some people are born that way. A dyslexic person's brain and eyes do not work together so easily as other people's do, and so they sometimes see things backwards. A dyslexic person has a hard time telling right from left."

"Reuben can't write neatly," Laura said. "And he's always spelling words wrong. Sister Margie said she will bring a treat to school for our class if we all get a hundred in spelling on the same day, and we never had a chance yet. Somebody always misses a word, and usually it's Reuben. And you know what happened today?" Laura's eyes grew wider.

"After our spelling test, the two other second grade boys were mean to Reuben in the bathroom! They laughed at him and called him a 'Backwards Boy,' and a 'Dummy'. They said it was all his fault that our class can't get a hundred in spelling. Reuben was so upset that he got sick, and threw up, and his mom had to come

get him. Then Sister Margie spanked both of the boys that mocked him!"

"And so she should," Mama said sternly. "Those boys were very, very naughty! You children can expect to get a hard spanking, too, if you ever mock, tease, or laugh at anyone less fortunate than you."

"What do you mean, 'less fortunate'?" Laura wondered.

"Well, I suppose that's a poor way to say what I mean," Mama sighed. "The Bible tells us that 'Whoso mocketh the poor reproacheth his Maker, and he that is glad at calamities shall not be unpunished.' We are not to mock the poor, or crippled, or the blind or the mentally retarded. Never poke fun at someone who is fat, or who stutters, or a person who has no friends, or somebody with a learning problem like Reuben's. Mocking others is a sin that must be very disgusting in the eyes of God."

"I remember when I was little," Timmy mused, "I mocked a little dwarf boy who came to visit our church. And Dad gave me the worst spanking of my life!" Timmy rubbed the seat of his pants, as if experiencing again the pain he had felt there.

"In the Bible, bears gobbled up forty-two children who mocked Elisha for being bald," Peter reminded Laura with a menacing growl. "Never, never mock somebody who is different!"

"Peter, the Bible doesn't say the bears *ate* those children," Mama corrected. "It says they 'tare them.' But that should be enough to show us what God thinks of mocking! God made all of us, and He makes each person the way they are for a purpose. We need to accept others and respect them just as God made them. Reuben may not have been created with a mind that finds it easy to write and spell, but I'm sure that God gave him other talents."

The next morning in school, Laura watched Reuben closely at first. Would he still be feeling sick? Was he going to act mad at the other boys who had mocked him? But Reuben seemed to be just as cheerful and friendly as ever, so Laura's attention soon moved to other things.

Lunchtime came, and while the children were eating their meal, Sister Margie brought some papers to the copier machine at the back of the classroom.

"What are you making, Teacher?" Laura asked, full of curiosity. "This is a pattern for our art project today," Sister Margie answered with a smile. "Next Sunday will be Mother's Day, and I want each of you to make a Mother's Day basket to take home."

"Goodie, goodie!" cried Laura and her friends. "That will be fun!" They turned in their seats to watch as Sister Margie turned on the photocopier and placed her pattern under the lid. The quiet hum of the machine began, and the little girls went back to their lunches.

Suddenly the peaceful hum was interrupted by a nasty rattling sound! Seventeen little heads whirled around to see what was the matter. That noise was coming from the copier! No more papers slid down the chute, but a red warning light was blinking ominously on the machine's front panel. Sister Margie's face wore a panicky expression. She hurried to switch the copier off, and then stood there looking at the machine as if it were a snake ready to strike.

"What happened, Teacher?" a chorus of little voices wondered.

"I don't know," Sister Margie replied, sounding worried. "Something is wrong with the copier. Oh, I wish Brother Ken was here! His class went on a field trip today, and I don't know much about fixing copiers."

"Then, can't we make our Mother's Day baskets?" asked Sarah Beth in a small, hurt voice.

"Oh, no! Can't we?" Laura and Jennifer echoed.

"I don't see how," Sister Margie said sadly. "I only had a few copies made before the machine quit working, and I don't know how to fix it."

"Maybe *I* can, Teacher," Reuben spoke up from the other side of the room.

Sister Margie turned around, surprised.

Reuben was out of his seat and coming over to the copier table. "I think I know what's wrong," he said confidently. "Was it *this* light blinking, right here?"

"Yes, that's the one," Sister Margie agreed.

"Well, that means there's some paper jammed up inside," the boy told her. "My dad's copier did that same thing last week, and I watched him fix it."

All Reuben's classmates watched breathlessly as he removed the front of the copier. *Will Reuben really be able to fix a machine, just like a man?* Laura wondered.

Now that the front panel was open, the class could see a bewildering array of knobs, wheels, wires, and pulleys. "*I* wouldn't dare touch any of that stuff," Sister Margie said apprehensively. "Are you sure you know what to do, Reuben?"

"Yes, this copier looks almost exactly like ours inside," Reuben assured her. He reached in under the mechanism and pulled out a wad of crumpled, creased paper. "See? this was stuck in the cassette brush," he said, holding it up. "Now I'll push the reset button and put the front cover back in place, and then it will work. I hope so, anyway!" Reuben added, smiling shyly.

Sure enough, the copier was soon humming again! Page after page of neat copies slid down the chute. Reuben had saved the day, and his friends looked at him with new respect.

"You're pretty smart about machines," Paul told him admiringly.

"Aw, well, I just like to watch my dad and learn all I can," Reuben said.

Just wait till I tell Mama what happened today! Laura thought. *Mama was right — God did give Reuben other talents. When he was fixing that copier, he didn't look much like a "backwards boy."*

9

A Stitch In Time
Proverbs 19:20

"Sharon, I'd like you to do the ironing this afternoon," Mama told her oldest daughter as the children enjoyed their after-school snack. "Be sure that you watch for loose buttons or anything else that might need mending. I believe your blue school dress has part of it's hem loose, so you'd better stitch it up right away."

"Oh, dear," Sharon sighed. "Mending is such an unpleasant chore!"

Mama smiled. "Well, Sharon, it's just one of those things which need to be taken care of," she said. "If we take care of problems while they are small, we can save a lot of time and trouble later on. As Benjamin Franklin is supposed to have said, '*A stitch in time saves nine!*'"

Sharon hummed a tune as she swished the

hot iron back and forth. Ironing was fun! She enjoyed smoothing out every wrinkle, and hanging up the crisp, fresh dresses and shirts. *If only I didn't have to do any mending,* she thought. Today there were no loose buttons on her brothers' shirts, no torn places in their pants. . . only that one troublesome skirt hem of her own!

I know what I'll do, Sharon decided. *It isn't worth threading a needle just to fix one dress. I'll just* pin *my hem into place now, and sew it some other day!* Hurrying over to Mama's sewing cabinet, Sharon pulled a long straight pin from the plump red-tomato pincushion. Carefully she pushed the pin through her dress hem: in and out, in and out again. There! Now the hem was secured, and the pin was hardly visible.

"You had better do what Mama said!" Sharon's conscience nagged her. *"Mama told you to sew that hem!"* But the young girl lightheartedly ignored her inner warnings. *This way was so much quicker!* she thought as she carried her load of clean clothes upstairs to put them away.

The next morning, Sharon pulled out that same blue dress from the closet and put it on, forgetting all about her hasty pin job. She ate breakfast, helped to pack the school lunches, and sat listening thoughtfully as Dad read aloud the morning's Scripture portion from the *Daily Light*. Later, at school, she went gladly over to the first and second graders' room to help Sister Margie.

The teacher directed Sharon to answer a question for Sarah Beth.

"I can't figure out how to do this Math," the first-grader whispered bashfully, looking up at Sharon. Smiling, Sharon knelt down beside the little girl's desk and began to patiently explain. A minute passed, then another, and Sharon moved one knee to bring it closer to the child's desk.

"*Ouch!*" A cry of pain burst from Sharon's lips, and her whole body jerked as if she had been stricken suddenly by an unseen hand. All the children raised their heads and stared curiously at Sharon.

"Is something wrong, Sharon?" Sister Margie asked, looking at her young helper in surprise.

"My pin!" Sharon moaned, struggling to her feet. "I knelt on a pin, and it broke off in my knee!" Her face was white with pain as she turned up the hem of her skirt. Sure enough, part of the pin was gone!

Sister Margie hurried over and helped Sharon to the nearest empty seat. Turning up the skirt hem, she inspected the broken straight pin. "How long *was* this pin?" she wondered.

"It was an extra long one," Sharon replied faintly. "Maybe an inch and a half, and now there's less than an inch left. Oooh, it hurts!"

"But there's no blood on your knee," the teacher observed. "I can't find any mark at all." Going back to Sarah Beth's desk, Sister Margie made a careful search of the floor. "Stay in your seats, children, but look all around you on the floor," she told her students. "I hope we can find the other piece of that pin!"

But her hope was in vain. The missing piece was nowhere in sight.

"It's *in* my knee!" Sharon insisted painfully. "I felt it snap off, and oh! it hurts whenever I move!"

"I'm afraid we will need to call your mother. If that pin is really in your knee, you will need to see a doctor," Sister Margie said regretfully.

"I guess so," Sharon whispered. A few tears welled up in her eyes and spilled over, in spite of her effort to keep them back. She tried to be brave, but the painful moments of waiting seemed endless before Mama finally arrived.

"Oh, Mama!" Sharon sobbed as they drove to the clinic. "If only I had *sewed* my skirt hem, instead of pinning it with that dreadful pin! I never imagined something like this could happen."

"Neither did I," Mama admitted. "It sounds impossible, for a pin to break off in your knee without leaving a mark. But since it hurts so badly, we had better take an X-ray to be sure."

At the clinic, a wheelchair was brought out

to the car for Sharon. An injection finally began to dull that terrible pain in her knee, and X-ray pictures were taken.

"Well, there it is," a white-coated technician said briskly at last, spreading out the X-ray negatives for Sharon and Mama to look at. With one fingernail, she pointed to the whitish sliver of metal visible against the bone. "You've really done it this time, Miss! That pin went right into your kneecap. One of the doctors will have to remove it."

The next few hours were a haze of pain and confusion for Sharon. The smells of antiseptic and medicine made her head swim, and so did the horrible buzz of the electric tool that the surgeon used to cut into her kneecap.

"How much money is all this going to cost, Mama?" the fifteen-year-old wondered apprehensively when they were finally in the car and on their way home.

"Over a thousand dollars," Mama replied softly.

"Oh, Mama!" Sharon cried out in horror. "And it was all my fault! You *told* me to mend my hem. If only I had listened!" Fresh tears ran down her pale cheeks.

Mama patted her daughter's hand. "Don't worry, Sharon. We all make mistakes," she comforted. "Let's just be thankful it wasn't any worse. Being careless has cost many people their lives! I don't think you will ever be careless about mending again."

Sharon did not return to school the next day, and that afternoon Laura came home full of excitement. "Guess what Sarah Beth did today," she told Sharon, giggling. "She was sitting in her desk just crying and crying. When Sister Margie asked what was wrong, she said 'They cut Sharon's leg off!'" She didn't understand that the doctor only cut your knee *open*. But all the girls in our class say we will never, never use pins in our clothes!"

Neither will I, Sharon thought wearily as her little sister bounced cheerfully away. Reaching across her sore, swollen knee, which was resting on a soft pillow, Sharon retrieved her Bible from the end table beside the couch. Languidly she flipped through the pages, looking for something inspiring to read.

"Hear counsel, and receive instruction!" the words seemed to reach out and catch Sharon's eye. "Hear counsel, and receive instruction," she read again. "Hear counsel, and receive instruction, that thou mayest be wise in thy latter end." Proverbs 19, verse 2d.

Well, I sure wish I had done what this verse says! Sharon thought. *If only I had listened to Mama's counsel, and obeyed her instruction, when she told me to mend my dress promptly.* "A stitch in time saves nine," *she said, and I didn't listen! I thought I knew a better way.*

A sudden idea struck Sharon. *I wonder. . .* "Mama!" she called. "How many stitches did the doctor put in my knee? Do you know?"

"I believe he said *nine* stitches," Mama called back from the next room. "Why do you wonder?"

Sharon only smiled grimly to herself. *"A stitch in time saves nine!"* Next time I'll *"hear counsel, and receive instruction,"* she thought.

10

What Would Jesus Do?
Ephesians 5:1

"After you multiply these two numbers, you must write your answer here," Sister Joy explained patiently. "Always move each row one place to the left, like this . . ."

Third-grader Linda was having trouble understanding her math work, so Sister Joy was giving her some extra help during recess. All the other middle-grade children were outside sledding on the snowy hill beside the school, and their teacher could plainly hear the happy shouts of their fun.

Suddenly, though, Sister Joy heard another sound. The heavy door at the other end of the hallway opened and closed again with an almost secretive click. Somebody was coming in, but why were they so quiet? There was a soft thump as that somebody removed his boots, and finally a figure appeared at the classroom door.

Sister Joy looked up. She saw Timmy walking slowly over to his desk, and she could tell at a glance that he was unhappy about something. He did not look up, but avoided the teacher's eye as he sat down.

"Are you cold, Timmy?" the teacher inquired.

"No," Timmy said shortly.

"Is everything going all right outside?" Sister Joy asked him.

The boy said nothing, but a telltale flush of crimson spread from his neck to his face.

"Timmy, what happened?" the teacher asked in a no-nonsense tone.

"Uh, some of the boys are pretending to shoot at each other," Timmy mumbled. "They point their fingers at each other and shoot, and then they roll off their sleds and play dead. I told them we shouldn't, and they just laughed at me. Eugene said, 'You're a little bit flaky, Timmy!'"

Timmy was trying to keep the tears from welling up in his eyes, but Sister Joy could tell his feelings had been hurt by his friend's words. With a sigh, the teacher moved over to the window where she could see her class. Yes, several of the boys seemed to be playing a 'war' game, just as Timmy said.

They all know they aren't supposed to do that! Sister Joy mourned inwardly. *Now what shall I do? Maybe I had better go out there . . . But they must learn to do what's right even when the teacher isn't with them. How shall I help them understand? They must* want *to do the right thing!*

Sister Joy sent up a brief, silent prayer for wisdom. Then she turned away from the window and walked over to Timmy. "I'm glad you wanted to do what was right, Timmy," she told him, patting his shoulder approvingly. "Now we need to help your friends understand, too, why they shouldn't pretend to shoot each other. You can help them want to do the right thing. I'd like you to go back and ask them this question: *'What do you think Jesus would do if He were you?'*

"You don't need to tell them that you told the teacher what they were doing. Just ask them, 'What would Jesus do?' I will be here at the window watching, and we will see what happens."

A spark of hope lit his eyes as Timmy stood up and made his way out of the classroom again. *What would Jesus do?* the words of his teacher rang through his mind. Timmy knew what Jesus would do if He were Timmy Miller! Jesus would forgive His friends, and try again to help them do what was right.

Timmy's boots and coat were soon on, and he came marching bravely up the snowy hill.

"Hey! Here comes Preacher Timmy!" Eugene called out as he approached. "Are you ready to play with us again?"

"Well, I want to ask you one thing first,"

Timmy replied in a clear, firm voice. "What would Jesus do if He were here?"

There was silence, and Timmy looked around at his friends. Frank and Philip looked ashamed. Jabez and Darwin sat on their sleds, with their eyes on their feet as they scuffled them in the snow.

"Aw, we're just playing. We weren't shooting anybody for real," Eugene argued.

"But Jesus wouldn't even *play* he was killing anyone!" Timmy challenged him.

"Okay, we'll stop," Frank announced. "What shall we play instead?"

"Let's play that we are rescuing people who are lost in the mountains," suggested Philip. "That's something Jesus would do."

The others gladly agreed, and soon the sleds were darting to and fro again, loaded with happy laughing boys.

Sister Joy, as she watched from the window, was happy too. She could see that the 'war' was over and peace had come to the little group of boys on the hillside, because they were trying to follow Jesus.

"Be ye therefore followers of God, as dear children;" the teacher quoted softly as she turned back to see how Linda was doing with her multiplication.

All our choices about doing what is right will be easy to make, if we just try to do what Jesus would do, she mused. "Be ye therefore followers of God, as dear children!" Ephesians 5:1.

11

My Heart Says Amen
Psalm 116:15 & James 5:14 -16

Mama heard the front door open, and looked up from her sewing machine. *Why, the children are home from school,* she thought. *But they are so quiet! Something must have gone wrong!*

"Welcome home, children," Mama smiled, as she looked questioningly from one face to another. Peter and Timmy looked sober. Sharon's face was pale, with traces of recent tears. Laura was the first one to speak.

"Mama! Marie Stutzman has a big, bad sickness, and she might die!" the little girl said bluntly.

"Marie?" Mama gasped. Turning to Sharon, she looked searchingly at her oldest daughter.

Another tear trickled down Sharon's cheek. "Marie didn't come to school yesterday or today," she said in a small voice. "Now they say she has leukemia. I knew she didn't feel very good this fall, but nobody knew. . . She told me on Monday that she had another doctor appointment. But why didn't she tell me what was wrong? Marie was my best friend!"

"Maybe they just found out what was wrong yesterday, too," Mama told her gently. "Is her cancer very advanced?"

"It's the very worst kind of leukemia, and the doctor says it's too late for chemotherapy," Sharon replied brokenly. "They say she might only have a few weeks to live!" Dropping into her mother's sewing chair, Sharon put her head down on her arms and wept.

Sunnyside School was an unusually quiet place during the next couple of days. Groups of girls and boys stood talking in hushed, serious voices. It was hard to concentrate on their usual studies, when Marie's empty desk was always there to remind them of the startling truth. Marie had always been a cheerful, calm, steady girl, friendly to all. The whole school would miss her!

"We all have special prayer for Marie every day," Laura reported at the supper table the next evening. "Tomorrow all the big children in Sharon and Peter's class are supposed to take a little present for Marie, and make a Sunshine Box."

"And we are going to go over to Marie's house tomorrow afternoon, to sing for her," Sharon added. To herself she thought, *I hope I can sing without crying!*

At a quarter till two on the following afternoon, Brother Ken's class crowded into two vans for a short drive to the Stutzman home.

Marie was sitting in a recliner chair in their living room, looking pale but cheerful. She greeted her school friends eagerly.

"We want to sing four or five songs for you," Brother Ken told her after a few minutes of conversation. "Do you have any you would like to choose?"

"Please sing number 365," Marie answered softly. "'My Heart Says Amen to Thy Will.' I've always liked that one, and especially now!"

Sharon's eyes blurred with unshed tears as she turned the pages of the hymnal. With an effort, she kept her voice steady.

... Though my plans and my hopes may seem
blighted,
I will love Thee and trust in Thee still;
For I know all is well that Thou doest,
And my heart says Amen to Thy will.

Yes, my heart says Amen to Thy will, Lord,
And I know that Thou lovest me still,
While I bow low in humble submission
And my heart says Amen to Thy will. . .

The class sang in their clear young voices. Marie's eyes were closed, and she smiled as her friends went on to sing several more of their familiar hymns. *She looks so peaceful,* Sharon thought, *as if her heart really does say "Amen" to God's will . . .*

"Isn't there *anything* the doctors can do to fix Marie?" Timmy questioned that evening at the supper table.

"The doctor told her parents that he didn't think they would have any success with the usual treatments anymore," Sharon replied. "Marie has been drinking carrot juice and taking different herbs and vitamins from the health food store. Maybe that will help her."

"God could still heal Marie, too," Dad said gravely. "We need to keep praying that His will be done. Marie and her parents have asked for anointing, as the Bible teaches. Tomorrow the ministers will go and anoint Marie, while our whole church prays."

Later, Dad called Sharon into his office. "When Marie asked to be anointed, she also had another special request," he told Sharon. "She asked if *you* may come along and be present for the anointing service, since you are such a close friend. Would you like to do that?"

A shiver of excitement ran up Sharon's spine. Of course she would! "Yes, I will," she managed to say, "if you think that would be all right."

Dad put his arm around Sharon's shoulders in a loving hug. "I know this has been a difficult time for you, Honey," he said softly. "Keep trusting in God, even when we can't understand His will! God loves Marie more than you do, and whether she lives or dies, she is His."

"People sometimes get healed when they are anointed, don't they?" Sharon asked hopefully.

"Yes, many times they do," her father answered. "I have seen and heard of many real miracles. And other times, God doesn't heal a person's body, but He gives them a spiritual blessing instead. He takes away their fear and pain, and gives them grace to bear their sickness. We cannot demand physical healing from God. Always, we must be surrendered to His will!"

"It would be hard for me to give up Marie," Sharon said huskily. "We have been friends ever since we were very little girls, and we've always done things together. Last year we were baptized together. And now . . ." she could say no more.

"Keep on praying, and your faith will be strengthened through this," Dad told her lovingly. "Perhaps God will heal Marie. If not, you can still rejoice that your friend will be in heaven with Jesus."

The following evening, a solemn little group of people gathered in the Stutzman's home. Marie's parents stood at her bed side, together with Brother John, the bishop; Dad Miller, and two other elders of the church.

"We have met together in obedience to God's

Word, and by our sister's request," Brother John said softly. "Let us read together from the fifth chapter of James, verses 14 to 16:

'Is any sick among you? Let him call for the elders of the church; and let them pray over him, anointing him with oil in the name of the Lord: and the prayer of faith shall save the sick, and the Lord shall raise him up; and if he have committed sins, they shall be forgiven him. Confess your faults one to another, that ye may be healed. The effectual fervent prayer of a righteous man availeth much,'

he read aloud in his deep, firm voice. "Brothers and sisters, we believe that God's Word is still true today. We want to pray His blessing on our young sister, Marie, and ask for healing according to God's will. First, let us be sure we are meeting the conditions in God's word by confessing our faults one to another. Does anyone have something to say?"

"I must ask God's forgiveness for my bitter feelings about Marie's illness," Marie's mother said softly. "I want to trust that God's will is best."

"And I spoke impatiently to my children before I came here tonight," one of the ministers confessed sadly. "I am sorry, and I will apologize to my family too. I don't want my sin to stand in the way of God's blessing!'"

When everyone felt ready and clear before God, Brother John opened a small bottle of special oil. All the ministers laid their hands on Marie's head in prayer, as Brother John anointed her with oil in the name of the Lord. Sharon stood breathlessly waiting in her corner nearby, her head bowed with reverence. Surely, God Himself was in the room with them!

For a few minutes there was silence, as every head bowed in worship. Brother John was the first to speak. "How do you feel, Sister Marie?" he asked tenderly.

"I still feel weak, but the pain is gone," Marie said clearly. "I believe God spoke to me and told me that I will be healed in heaven. I'm ready to go, and I'm not afraid."

In heaven! Sharon thought. *So Marie knows she is going to die!* But as Sharon stood with bowed head she felt only peace. Her heart, like Marie's, would say "Amen" to God's will.

Two weeks later, the Miller family stood beside Marie's open grave. Marie's parents and brothers and sisters sat on folding chairs, surrounded by hundreds of their Christian friends. A chilly December wind rattled the bare branches of the trees around the small church cemetery. But there was sunshine, too, streaming down from an opening in the gray clouds!

Sharon, Peter, Timmy and Laura moved forward to stand with all the other students of

Sunyside School. The children had been asked to sing while the grave was being filled.

"Mommy, why are they doing that?" Sharon heard a small boy ask his mother as the men with shovels began to cover Marie's casket.

"Marie has gone to heaven, and she won't need that old body anymore," the mother told her child softly. "We put it into the ground, and cover it with earth, just like when we plant seeds in the garden. God will give Marie a new, perfect body in heaven!"

Brother Ken nodded to the school children, and fifty-five young voices began to sing.

> 'When I pass to that heavenly country,
> And my soul with its glory doth thrill,
> This forever shall be my rejoicing
> That my heart said Amen to Thy will.'

Marie lived fifteen years on this earth, Sharon thought, *but she will spend eternity with the Lord. She can forever rejoice that she was obedient to God's will.* "Precious in the sight of the Lord is the death of His saints!"

> 'Yes, my heart says Amen to Thy will, Lord,
> And I know that Thou lovest me still,
> While I bow low in humble submission
> And my heart says Amen to Thy will . . .'

12

What's In a Name?
Proverbs 22:1

When the Miller children stepped out of the school van one Monday morning, Frank was waiting for Timmy with excitement written all over his face. "Timmy!" he reported in a loud whisper, "there's a new boy in our class this morning!"

"I knew there was going to be a new family," Timmy replied. "Is there a fourth-grade boy? Is he nice?"

"I don't know yet," Frank replied as the two boys entered the school. "He has a funny name, but I forgot it already."

Quickly Timmy hung up his coat and placed his lunch box on the shelf. Hurrying as fast as he could go without running, he followed Frank down the hallway to their classroom. The new boy stood alone in the back of the room, looking at Sister Joy's aquarium.

My, his hair is red! Timmy thought. *He has the reddest hair I've ever seen on a boy!* Slowly, Timmy and Frank walked over to join the new boy at the aquarium.

"Hi! My name is Timmy Miller," Timmy introduced himself politely. "What's yours?"

"I'm Darwin Shank," the boy replied. "I'm in fourth grade."

"Darwin?" Timmy repeated, surprised. A gleam of mischief came into his eyes. "Do you believe in evolution, Darwin?" he asked teasingly.

The red-haired boy bristled like a feisty young rooster. Obviously he had heard this question before. "No! Of course I don't!" he snapped angrily. "Do you?"

"No, I was just asking," Timmy explained hastily," because of your name. You know, Darwin was the man who . . ."

"Yes, I know," Darwin interrupted rudely. "But I wouldn't talk about other people's names if I were you. You have plenty of *really* weird names in this school!" He looked at the group of boys that was gathering around. "Like *Micah*, and *Jabez*," he said looking at two third-grade boys. "Whoever heard of somebody named *Jabez*? And *Eeyeww-geene*," he added, drawing out each syllable scornfully. "I call that a sissy name!" Now it was Eugene's turn to look offended.

"Jabez was a righteous man in the Bible,"

81

his namesake spoke up defensively. "I'd rather be named after a good, Bible man than a wicked evolutionist like Darwin!"

The new boy looked almost ready to cry. "But I *wasn't* named for Charles Darwin, the evolution man," he insisted. "My parents named me Darwin because it's a family name. My uncle is named Darwin, and my grandpa, and *his* Grandpa was named Darwin before anybody knew about evolution. I can't help it that my name is the same as . . ."

Timmy felt uncomfortable and guilty. He shouldn't have teased this boy about his name, on his first day in a new school!

"I'm sorry I made fun of your name, Darwin," he said quickly. "That wasn't nice of me. Let's be friends, okay?"

No one had seen Sister Joy standing on the edge of the group of boys, until she spoke. "Boys, you must never make fun of *anyone's* name," the teacher spoke earnestly. "That is very unkind. Nobody has the privilege of choosing their name, so the name you have is something you cannot help.

"There is a way you can *make* a name for yourself, though," she smiled at the boys. Proverbs 22:1 tells us that 'A good name is rather to be chosen than great riches.' This verse isn't talking about the name your parents gave you; it's talking about a name you can choose! Your 'good name' is your reputation, the way people think of you. If you are diligent, honest, and true; if you are friendly and kind, then people will think of good things when they think of your name. That is the best way to have a good name, isn't it? And now it's time for the bell, so let's go take our seats.

"Darwin, you will sit at the end of this row, behind Timmy."

Timmy smiled at the new boy, and Darwin smiled back. *After this, I will be more careful to be kind,* Timmy thought. *I want to have a good name!*

13

The "Two-Faced Apples"
Psalm 15:1-3

"Well, Sharon, what happened in *your* class today?" Dad Miller inquired as he speared a baked potato with his fork.

Sharon leaned back from her plateful of supper and began to laugh. "Oh, it's so funny!" she exclaimed. "The two-faced apples finally turned on each other."

"Two-faced apples? What do you mean?" Timmy pricked up his ears at once.

"When someone is two-faced, that means they are nice when they talk *to* you, but nasty when they talk *about* you," Sharon explained. "Like an apple that's good on one side and rotten on the other. And we have two girls in our class who were just like that, until today."

"This really doesn't sound funny," Mama

said with a sober look at her oldest daughter.

"Oh, I don't mean to gossip," Sharon replied hastily. "But Rachel and Leanna have been acting like two-faced apples to each other all year so far, and today it caught up with them. They've learned their lesson, I hope, and it should be a lesson to all of us."

"Tell us what happened, then," Dad encouraged Sharon.

"Well, Rachel and Leanna have been calling each other 'best friends' this year," Sharon began, "but it hasn't been the right kind of friendship. The main thing they enjoyed doing together was gossiping about all the rest of us! They would stand together whispering and giggling whenever they could, saying unkind things about others. They talked about how shabby some people's houses were, and how other people think they're so smart to have a new house. And they would criticize the teacher, and make fun of anybody in class who was fat, or clumsy, or just happened to make a mistake during the day.

"And besides all this, they weren't even loyal to each other! They would say nice things to each other's face, but then start running each other down when they were speaking to other girls. Leanna would compliment Rachel on her pretty new dress, but when Rachel wasn't around she whispered to me, 'Did you *see* Rachel's new dress? How can she stand to wear such a funny color!' Rachel told Leanna what a *good cook* her mother was, but later I heard her giggling as she told some other girls about the 'strange, weird food' she'd been served at Leanna's house.

"We all knew there was trouble coming, and it came today. Leanna's family just traded in their car for a nice 8-passenger mini-van, and it happens to be nearly the same kind as Rachel's family has. Rachel was all smiles when she talked with Leanna about it. 'Isn't this *great*? Our families can have matching vans!" Rachel bubbled, and she practically hugged Leanna.

"Later, though, when several of us girls were walking through the church auditorium on our way back to class, Rachel had a completely different tune. 'Leanna thinks she's so smart!' she hissed spitefully. 'Her family are just a bunch of copycats. Why did they have to get a van like ours?'

"At that moment, Leanna herself rose up from behind the benches, where she had been sitting on the floor checking some papers for Sister Margie. None of us had seen her, but she had heard every word. Her face was pale, and then turned very red. 'Rachel, you are a two-faced apple! she cried. '*Some* friend you turned out to be, you back-biter!' she snapped angrily. Rachel began talking back just as angrily, and then suddenly Brother Ken was beside them.

"'Leanna and Rachel, you come to the office with me," he said firmly, and led them away. In a minute he was back and told me to ring the bell. 'The whole class may have a study period now,' he said briefly, and left again.

"It was a long, long time before Brother Ken brought Rachel and Leanna back from the office. They both had tear-stained faces, but it was obvious that they had forgiven one another and resolved to do better in the future."

"I hope Brother Ken told them that people who will talk about others *to* you, will usually talk the same way to others *about* you," Mama said gently. "That is human nature. I trust Rachel and Leanna will break their habit of backbiting, and have a true, worthwhile friendship from now on."

"The Bible often mentions backbiting, gossip, and slander," Dad told his family. "God wants us to be humble in our attitudes toward others, and not talk unkindly about them. Psalm 15 tells us about a godly person's character," Dad continued, reaching for a Bible.

'Lord, who shall abide in thy tabernacle? who shall dwell in thy holy hill? He that walketh uprightly, and worketh righteousness, and speaketh the truth in his heart. He that backbiteth not with his tongue, nor doeth evil to his

neighbor, nor taketh up a reproach against his neighbour.' —
Dad read aloud.

"So, children, let's be sure we always speak kindly; *to* people and *about* people. We want to be pleasing to the Lord," he concluded. "That way we will never be two-faced apples!"

14

The Substitute Teacher
Ephesians 6:6, 7

The afternoon was nearly over when Brother Ken made his announcement. "Boys and girls," he told his students, "tomorrow I need to be away from school for the day, so you will have a substitute teacher."

Instantly, all eighteen of the upper-grade students were staring at him in surprise. Joshua raised his hand first and asked the question that was in everybody's mind. "*Who* will our substitute be?"

"The school board has asked Leanna's grandmother, Sister Martha Troyer, to substitute for the day," Brother Ken replied. "Sister Martha has kindly agreed to take my place. I'm sure she will do the job well." The teacher paused and smiled at his class, but his eyes were stern as he went on.

"I expect all of you to behave yourselves

properly and responsibly, to make her job as pleasant as possible. You will address your substitute as *Sister* Martha, just like any regular teacher. And you will obey all of the usual rules, just as when I am here. In fact, I want you to be *extra* obedient and cooperative, and help the day go as smoothly as possible. Being a substitute teacher is not an easy task, and I don't want anyone to make it any harder for her with any discipline problems!" Brother Ken looked earnestly around at his students, and Peter found himself nodding in agreement.

But the next morning started out all wrong! When Peter stepped out of the van at the school house door, he saw a huddled group of his classmates looking at a box made of plywood. "What do you have there?" Peter called, running over to join the group.

"It's Joseph's pet!" Henry answered in a mysterious tone, moving aside to let Peter into the circle. "Have you ever seen it, Peter?"

"Oh, yes, I saw it when we went to Joseph's house for dinner," Peter chuckled. "Why did you bring it to school, Joseph?"

"Shhh!" Joseph winked at Peter. "Keep quiet! We're going to show it to our substitute, and see how high she'll jump!"

Peter looked doubtful, and Sharon, who had come to peer over his shoulder, was shocked. "Boys! you shouldn't," she scolded. "What if Sister Martha faints, or has a heart attack? She's a grandma!"

"Don't be so worried," Henry blustered. "We asked Leanna first, and she doesn't think her grandma will get *that* scared. It will be just good fun."

"We're gonna wait until everyone's here," Joseph explained, "and then we will carry the box in and ask Sister Martha if she wants to see my pet. Then everyone can watch what she'll do."

When the bell rang, all the upper graders trooped into their classroom with an air of eager expectancy.

"Good morning, boys and girls," their substitute teacher greeted. Her eyes went to the wooden box in Joseph's hand. "What do you have there?" she smiled in a friendly way.

"It's my pet," Joseph smiled innocently. "I brought it to school this morning. Want to see?" Carefully, he placed the plywood box on the teacher's desk and unfastened the clasp. Swinging open the hinged door at one end of the box, Joseph peered into the dark interior. "It must be hiding back in its nest," he said, frowning. Turning the box so that the open end was facing Sister Martha, he bent to look through a wire-covered window at one side of the box. At the same time, he rapped sharply with his knuckles on the box's top.

Zzzzip! With the release of Joseph's hidden spring, a long cylindrical blur of fur shot from the box directly into Sister Martha's lap.

"OOH!" gasped the startled lady. "What-what *is* it?" She looked down at the motionless 'creature' in her lap, as the children watched her breathlessly. What would the substitute do? Was she going to scream? faint? get angry?

But Martha Troyer had raised four boys of her own, and was made of sterner stuff than that. "Why, it's only a foxtail, isn't it?" she observed in a voice that was almost steady again. "How do you make it jump?"

Joseph and his friends hastened to explain the spring mechanism which held the foxtail. Lifting the top of the box, they showed Sister Martha how the foxtail could be fastened into place. Then they demonstrated how the spring released when someone pounded on the box, making the foxtail shoot out.

"Very interesting! That's quite an invention," Sister Martha said. "Now just slide it here under my desk, Joseph. It's time for classes to begin."

Sister Martha took charge of the day with calm authority, and most of the pupils relaxed. But Joseph, Peter, and a few of the other boys had felt rather disappointed by her lack of reaction to the foxtail trick. *She's pretty smart,* Peter thought, with a mixture of admiration and resentment. *Wonder if we can trick her some other way?*

And so it happened after first recess, when the time came for the teacher to ring the bell on her desk and call the class to order, the bell wouldn't ring! With a puzzled look, Sister Martha tapped the bell again. Still there was no sound. Without a word, the substitute teacher picked up the bell and turned it upside down. Scooping out with her fingers the wads of tissue paper that kept the bell from doing its job, she dropped them into the wastebasket; then she rang the bell as if nothing had happened.

Several of the boys had red faces, but Sister Martha made no comment. After a few minutes, a small folded piece of folded paper landed on Peter's desk. Cautiously, he opened it behind the cover of his history book. *I'm going to* hide *her old bell at noon!* the note read in Henry's scrawled writing. *Then what can she do?*

After noon recess, the bell was nowhere to be seen on the teacher's desktop. But Sister Martha didn't waste more than a moment looking for it, nor did she ask about the missing bell. "Everyone take your seats now," she spoke crisply. Then, picking up the story book from Brother Ken's desk, she began to read aloud as he usually did.

After story time, though, the eraser throwing began. The substitute teacher was at the blackboard with her back to the class, when the first pink rubber square sailed in a graceful curve across the room. *Plop*! It bounced off Janet's desk onto the floor. *Boinng!* A larger one rebounded from the wall. Every boy appeared to be busy at his work, but it wasn't long before two more erasers landed with a *plip! plip!* On the floor near the teacher's desk.

"Boys, whoever has thrown an eraser, come and pick them up," Sister Martha said sternly. Peter, Andy, Henry, and Joseph rose from their seats.

"I'm going to make a blow-gun next. Just watch!" Peter whispered as he passed Henry in the aisle. "What?" Henry whispered back, but Peter had already returned to his seat. Taking a sheet of notebook paper, Peter rolled it into a thin tube and scotch-taped the sides to hold it together. Then he carefully put the tube into his desk, and began making tiny paper pellets for ammunition. *You know you're doing wrong,* Peter's conscience whispered. *You should be* extra *good for the substitute teacher!* But Peter was so caught up in the excitement of "trying out" Sister Martha that he paid no attention to the warning voice.

Soon the teacher was standing at the blackboard again with her back to the class, and Peter pulled out his blowgun. Loading it with a couple of pellets, he aimed it at Joseph across the aisle. Fffft! he blew through the paper tube, shooting out the pellets with all the force he could manage. A quiet ripple of giggles spread among the boys and girls who had seen what happened! Sharon shook her head and frowned at her brother, but soon several more of the boys' desks had also turned into blowgun factories.

"Boys, we will have *no* pea-shooters, catapults, blow-guns or other such inventions during school," Sister Martha announced suddenly in a very definite voice. "I'm sure Brother Ken does not usually allow such an activity. And Joseph, I see that you are chewing gum. Does Brother Ken allow gum-chewing during class?"

Sheepishly Joseph shook his head.

"I didn't think so," the substitute replied. "Come up here and dispose of it in the wastebasket." Leanna's grandmother did not look like she was enjoying this day very much, and Peter began to feel miserable too. Really, school wasn't very much fun when people didn't follow the rules!

Brother Ken was in his usual place behind his desk the next morning.

"Boys and girls, you may turn to the sixth chapter of Ephesians for our devotional meditation," he said. "I will read aloud four verses:

'Servants, be obedient to them that are your masters according to the flesh, with fear and trembling, in singleness of your heart, as unto Christ; Not with eyeservice, as menpleasers; but as the servants of Christ, doing the will of God from the heart; With good will doing service, as to the Lord, and not to men: Knowing that whatsoever good thing any man doeth, the same shall he receive of the Lord, whether he be bond or free.'

"These verses tell us *why* we must be obedient, do the right thing, and follow the rules," Brother Ken told his students. "We must do right *from our heart,* as *unto the Lord.* If we do the right thing only when certain people are watching us, then we are missing the most important point. *God* sees us all the time, even when our parents and teachers don't! 'Not with eyeservice, as menpleasers,' the Scripture says. That means we don't do things right only for the eyes of certain people. We want to be 'servants of Christ, doing the will of God from our heart . . . as unto the Lord, and not unto men.'"

Brother Ken looked seriously at his students. "I am glad that most of you behaved yourselves properly yesterday when I wasn't here," he said. "But I was very disappointed to hear that a few of you did not. I had asked Sister Martha to write down the names of any pupils who did not behave, and she did so. Joseph, Henry, Andy, and Peter, you will stay in at recess and we will talk about the consequences of your actions."

At recess time, Brother Ken sat down with the four unhappy boys. "Well, boys, what would you do if you were the teacher, and some of your pupils took advantage of their substitute teacher?" he asked.

There was silence. Four guilty boys didn't know where to look or what to say!

"Each of you may take a small piece of scrap paper, and write down your answer to that question," the teacher said at last. When the boys had done so, Brother Ken studied the papers for a long moment. *We should stay in at recess some more,* two of the boys had written. *I would give them lots of sentences to write,* said another paper. *Apologize to Sister Martha,* the fourth paper added.

"Okay, boys, you have chosen your own punishments," the teacher said gravely. "You shall stay in for the rest of this recess, and all of noon hour. I want you to use that time to copy Ephesians 6:6 and 7 neatly on tablet paper, fifty times each. And also, each of you must make an apology to Martha Troyer, sometime this week. You may speak to her personally at church, call her on the telephone, or write her a letter. You boys were not behaving like gentlemen, when you played tricks on a lady old enough to be your grandmother! Tell her you are sorry you were disrespectful and disobedient when she was here at school."

Brother Ken stood up. "Take your Bibles and some clean sheets of paper now," he directed. "Writing these verses fifty times should help you commit them to your memory. This is the most important lesson you can learn during the school year: to do what is right for the sake of pleasing God! God always sees us, even when our parents can't . . . and even when there is a substitute teacher."

15

"Friendly Four" No More
Matthew 7:12

When Sharon walked into the girls' restroom at school one Friday morning during recess and saw Leanna standing alone by the sink, she knew that something was wrong. Leanna's blonde head drooped dejectedly, and even her back seemed to be bent with the weight of some heavy problem.

"Are you okay, Leanna?" Sharon wondered kindly as she squirted soap onto her hands. "I got paste all over my fingers while I was helping the first graders this morning. Guess I'm just as messy as they are!" she chattered in a friendly tone.

The younger girl barely managed a smile. "I wish I could help the little children," she said wistfully. "That might be easier than trying to get along with people my own age."

"Are you having problems today?" Sharon guessed sympathetically. "Would you like to talk about it?"

"Well, uh . . . I guess I have to apologize to some people, and I don't know how I'm going to start," Leanna mumbled. Then her face took on a defiant look. "Why can't we choose who we want to be friends with, anyway?" she exclaimed. "Rachel and Amy and Judy and I, we're good friends. We're the 'Friendly Four'! What's wrong with that?"

Sharon's own face was sober as she leaned against the sink. *"Lord, help me know what I should say,"* she breathed a silent prayer.

"But, Leanna, there are five of you girls in seventh grade," she began. "I guess there are *six* now, since the Shank family came back from the mission in Guatemala. It would be so much better if all six of you girls were friendly together, instead of making these exclusive cliques."

"But Lucinda Shank is so . . . well, she's just *different*," Leanna defended herself weakly. "Her clothes just don't look like the rest of us girls' clothes. And she talks funny sometimes. And she doesn't know how to play all the games we play, because she lived in Guatemala so long. And can you imagine," Leanna giggled mockingly. "She didn't know who the *'Miller Four'* singers were, when we mentioned them the other day. She wondered if they were *your* family!"

Sharon did not join in the other girl's laughter. "You can't expect Lucinda to know everything about life here right away," she said calmly. "I imagine *you* would be pretty 'different' too, if you suddenly moved to Guatemala now! Why don't you kindly help her to get acquainted with things, instead of pushing her away? Lucinda is a nice, kind Christian girl, and that is the most important thing."

"Well, you know . . . it's just more fun to be with my friends who are just like me," Leanna answered lamely. "Ruth is Lucinda's cousin, and she's kind of goody-goody anyway, so we just let her take care of Lucinda. They have each other, and the rest of us are the Friendly Four. What's wrong with that?" she demanded again. "There's nothing in the Bible about that, is there?"

"Yes, Leanna, there is," Sharon replied quietly. "The Bible says: *'Therefore all things whatsoever ye would that men should do to you, do ye even so to them!'* That's the Golden Rule. And it says, *'for this is the Law and the Prophets.'* The Golden Rule is the meaning of God's Law! Are you girls following the Golden Rule when you avoid Ruth and Lucinda, and snicker at them, and say unkind things about them? Just imagine how you would feel if you were Lucinda, and came to a new school where the other girls didn't accept you. Or how do you think Ruth feels, when you other girls push her away and leave her out?"

Leanna stared silently at the floor. "Judy was at my house overnight," she said at last. "We were . . . ah, we were talking about Ruth and Lucinda, and I guess we did talk too much. And we wrote some notes about them, too. Then my parents found the notes, and they talked to the other girls' parents, and I'm supposed to apologize to Ruth and Lucinda today. And my parents say we can't have the 'Friendly Four'! I don't know what to *do*," she finished sadly, looking up at Sharon.

Since Marie's death, Sharon had been the oldest girl at Sunnyside School; and now she felt very mature and responsible as she faced the troubled Leanna.

"I think I know why it's so hard for you to be a friend to Lucinda," Sharon told the younger girl gently.

"Why?" Leanna wondered.

"You're afraid," said Sharon, and smiled at the other girl's surprise. "Sometimes children are that way; they are afraid to be friends with anybody who is a little bit different. It's like they are scared people will think *they* are different, too. Or maybe they think being different is catching, like a disease."

"But that sounds silly," Leanna said, blushing a little.

"Yes, it is silly," Sharon replied. "Ruth and Lucinda are the very best kind of girls to have for friends. They are kind, true, and sensible, and they are fun to be with. They don't just giggle about boys all the time, either. You don't have to worry about apologizing to them, Leanna! They are the kind of girls who will forgive you without holding grudges, and be your friends. Just think how much more pleasant school will be, when you can all be friends together, instead of sneaking around and whispering in corners!"

"I suppose so," Leanna looked hopeful.

"Life is short," Sharon mused softly. "We can't afford to waste it being unkind. Look at Marie! She only lived fifteen years, and was gone suddenly. One day she was here at school, and . . . and then she never came back. But Marie was always kind and friendly to everyone! Marie tried to live like Jesus wants us to live, and now we can be sure that she is with the Lord."

Both girls' eyes stung with tears, for the memory of their departed classmate was fresh in everyone's mind.

Leanna squared her shoulders with determination. "Guess I'll go apologize like a big girl," she said bravely, trying to smile. "And I'll just have to tell the other girls that the 'Friendly Four' is over. From now on, we are all just *friends!*"

"Good for you," Sharon encouraged her. "That's what Marie would have done . . . and I'm sure it will please the Lord, too."

16

Just the Way I Am
Isaiah 64:8

One Friday afternoon, Sister Margie handed out clean, white sheets of drawing paper to each of her pupils.

"Today, children, I want each of you to draw a pair of animals," she told the class of first and second graders. "You may choose an animal, draw two of them on your paper, and color them as realistically as you can."

Reuben raised his hand. "Why are we supposed to draw a *pair* of animals?" he wondered.

The teacher smiled. "I'm planning to make a big picture of Noah's ark, to hang on the classroom wall," she explained. "Your pictures of animals will go up on the wall, too, as if they are marching toward the Ark. Won't that be a nice thing to show your mothers and fathers on Parents' Night?

"Now, I'd like to have each one of you draw a different kind of animal," Sister Margie went on. "Which animals do you choose? I'll write a list on the chalkboard, beside your name."

Hands began waving all around the classroom, as each child thought of the animal they wanted. "I'll do the lions!" Jason exclaimed. "I want the giraffes!" said Sarah Beth. "Ostriches!" Jennifer cried, and Michael spoke for the monkeys.

Laura felt a bit anxious. *What animal would be the easiest to draw?* she thought. *I can never draw any animal that looks like it should. Everyone will laugh at mine!*

At last Laura raised her hand. "I'll try the bears," she said timidly. *A bear shouldn't be too hard to draw . . . bears just look like big, furry lumps,* she decided.

When the paper was on her desk, Laura began to worry all over again. Such a clean, white paper! What if she made a mistake? Slowly, she drew a small round head and added pointy ears. Then she looked around to see what the other children were doing.

Across the aisle from Laura, Paul was sketching the figure of a horse. *My, he can really draw!* Laura thought admiringly. *All those pencil lines just take shape until you can see a real horse.* Paul's horse had everything: its neck arched proudly, the mane and tail flowed gracefully, and you could see rippling muscles and neat little hooves. The horse looked like it was galloping across the paper already!

Sadly, Laura turned back to her own paper. The bear she had started to draw looked much too small, so she erased it and started over. But no matter how hard she tried, Laura just couldn't make anything that looked like a bear.

"What are *those*, Laura?" Paul whispered as he walked by on his way back from the pencil sharpener.

Laura tried to cover the half-finished picture with her hands, but Paul stood on tiptoe and peeked between her fingers. *"Bears?!"* he scoffed. "Those look like turtles! Why don't you make their eyes down *here*," he said pointing, "instead of up on top their heads? And you should make claws on their feet, too."

"Paul, you must go quietly back to your seat," Sister Margie reminded him. Paul hurried to obey, and Laura bent over her bears again. She made the changes Paul had suggested, and then stared at her two bears. One was much bigger than the other, but Laura decided that one could be the father bear. *I guess I'll color them now*, she thought, and opened her desk to take out her crayons.

At last all the pictures were finished and hanging on the wall. Laura's classmates chattered and giggled as they stood in a group, admiring the rows of marching animals. "Paul's horses are the best!" one girl declared. "No,

Michael's monkeys are," Paul said modestly. Both the horses and the monkeys were very good. *I think those boys can draw better than the teacher, or even my daddy,* Laura thought. *But my bears are just the worst of all! Nobody will ever tell* me *that they like my picture.*

Laura was silent and miserable as she stood at the edge of the group. But suddenly she noticed something that made her stare, and a tiny giggle escaped her lips. "Look what Paul wrote at the bottom of his picture!" she exclaimed. Several children bent closer to look.

"That's not the right way to spell *horses,*" Laura said loudly. She felt much bigger now than she had a moment ago. Paul, the artist everyone admired, had made a mistake — and *she* had caught it ! "Look!" she exclaimed again. "He spelled *horses* with a 'c' instead of an 's'. H-O-R-C-E-S!"

"Well, so he did," Sister Margie said calmly, "and I missed it too. Here, Paul, you may erase that 'c' and change it to an 's'."

Laura felt very downhearted that evening after school, and she decided to tell her father about it.

"Daddy," she began, after climbing into his lap, "Why can some people draw things really well, and other people can't? It isn't fair."

Dad Miller smiled down at his little daughter. "Did you have a drawing lesson at school today?" he asked.

"Well, we all had to draw animals," Laura answered. "Everyone drew a different kind, and some of them were really nice! But I just can't draw anything that looks right. Paul said my bears looked like turtles," she finished sadly.

"Different people have different talents," Dad mused, giving Laura a comforting squeeze. "God didn't make us all the same! Some people are good at drawing, and some people have other skills."

"Paul drew horses, and he can draw much better than Sister Margie," said Laura. "But then, you know what he did? He spelled *horses* with a 'c', so it said *horces*. And he's a second grader. Even I know better than that, and I'm only in first grade!"

"So, Laura, do you see what that means?" Dad chuckled. "Even though drawing may not be your best talent, you have a talent for spelling. Paul is good at art, but finds writing and spelling harder to do. God made each one of us, and he gave us different talents for a special reason. We need to work hard and do our best, of course. You will grow better at drawing as you get older, and Paul will learn to write and spell! But we must also accept the talents God gave us, and be happy to say: 'God made me just the way I am!'

"Remember the time we went to Cousin Eric's pottery shop?" Dad went on, and Laura nodded. "Cousin Eric takes a lump of clay, and makes it into whatever he chooses. One lump of clay turns into a vase, and another into a pitcher, and another lump is made into a piggy-bank. Do you think that a clay piggy-bank ever says to Cousin Eric, 'Why did you make me like this? I want to be a pitcher!'"

"No, I'm sure they don't," Laura giggled.

"Some *people* behave that way, though," Dad pointed out. "Some people say, 'why did God make me the way I am? I'd rather have somebody else's talents!' But God is the potter, and we are the clay."

Dad reached for his Bible and turned to Isaiah 64:8.

"'But now, O Lord, thou art our father; we are the clay, and thou our potter; and we all are the work of thy hand,' he read aloud.

"So, remember, Laura! Do your best in everything, and learn all the skills you can. But always remember that God made you the person you are, with the talents you have. Always remember to say, 'Thank-you, God, for making me, just the way I am!'"

17

Peter and the In-Thing
Exodus 23:1 & 2

"Mom, I wish you would buy me some sardines for my lunch when you go to town," said Peter one morning at breakfast.

"Why, Peter! I thought you didn't like sardines," Mama replied in surprise.

"Well . . . uh, maybe they aren't so bad after all. I'd like to try some again," Peter answered sheepishly.

"I know why!" Sharon spoke up, laughing at her twelve-year-old brother. "Sardines are a big fad for the boys in our class right now. Most of the boys had sardines and crackers for lunch *every day* this week. *Pee-yew!*"

"So, Peter, you want sardines because they are the 'in thing' and you're feeling left out?" Mama observed, with a strange sort of smile.

"I'm tired of eating sandwiches like a girl, while the other boys eat sardines and crackers," Peter explained.

"Well, son, I hope you learn to enjoy sardines because *you* like them, not just to copy others," Dad told him. "It's nice to feel like part of a group, and to do wholesome things together with our friends. But we don't *have* to do what others are doing, and there are many times when we shouldn't. Wise people know how to be themselves and stand alone when that is necessary."

Dad looked at Peter's arms. "Peter, you must turn down your shirt sleeves, right now!" he said quietly but firmly. "A short sleeved shirt has sleeves that are short enough, without rolling them up any farther. Is that another 'in thing', to turn up your sleeves like that?"

"Some of the other boys do, I guess," Peter mumbled.

"Sardines may be a *harmless* fad, but this is not," Dad told him. "Rolling up your sleeves that are already short is foolish and immodest. We don't want to follow any fads or fashions that are foolish, immodest or dangerous. Christians will dress sensibly. We stay away from fads that show rebellion and folly, like walking around in untied shoes or wearing torn clothes on purpose."

That day at recess, Henry sidled up to Peter with a furtive look in his eyes. "See these?" he said in a low voice, holding up a pile of small thin cards in his hands.

"What are they?" Peter asked curiously.

"*You* know. Baseball cards," Henry whispered. Take a look, but don't let Brother Ken see you, or he'll *confisticate* them."

"*Confiscate* them, you mean," Peter chuckled. "Baseball cards aren't allowed at school. Where did you get these?"

"I bought them myself, when my mom wasn't looking," Henry snickered. "Lots of us boys have them, and the teacher doesn't know a thing. They're so much fun! You'd better get some too, Peter, if you aren't too chicken."

"I'll think about it," Peter said briefly, turning away from Henry. *But I won't need to think very long at all,* he sighed to himself. *I know what my parents would say about baseball cards!*

When Peter sat down at the breakfast table the very next morning, he stared wide-eyed at the cereal box in front of him.

FREE INSIDE!
FAMOUS OLYMPIC BASEBALL CARDS!

The advertisement was printed in bold red letters beside the colorful picture of a bowl of cereal.

Tipping the box, Peter poured a slow stream of little brown flakes into his dish. Holding the box up to eye-level, he peered in. Yes, there was something . . . he shook the box and tipped it again. *Crackle, thump!* Out slid a small packet wrapped in shiny cellophane. Yes, they actually were baseball cards. Peter held his breath,

looking cautiously around the kitchen. He was the first one at the table, and nobody was watching him except Beth in her high chair. *I could slip them into my pocket, and take them along to school!* he thought. *Should I?*

For a moment Peter struggled with temptation, but then his mother spoke from across the room. "Are there really baseball cards in that cereal box, Peter?" she asked. "If you find any, take them and throw them into the wastebasket before the other children see them."

"What's *wrong* with baseball cards, Mom?" Peter wondered as he dropped the tempting little packet into the trash.

"Baseball cards are like idols," Mama answered as she opened the refrigerator door. "When people pay so much honor and respect to the professional ball players of this world, it is like worshiping an idol. These sports stars are usually very ungodly men who live wicked lives, and we do not want them to be our children's heroes. Many children waste a lot of time and money collecting cards, just to keep up with their friends. We don't want that kind of thing to get started in our school."

Peter was quiet as he ate his cereal, but there was a struggle going on in his mind. *Why are my parents so strict?* he thought. *They are against every "in-thing". I'll look like a chicken if I'm the only one without baseball cards!*

Finally he spoke aloud the question that

was troubling him: "Is it always wrong to do what everybody else does?"

"Why, no, Peter, not necessarily," Dad replied. "There are many times when we *should* follow the example of others, especially our Christian friends. And there are times when it doesn't matter whether we do follow or whether we don't; we can make our own choice. But people who feel like they must copy their friends, no matter what, are asking for trouble. We don't want to be like ignorant sheep, who will follow the crowd right over a cliff or through the fence and onto a dangerous highway. Always think for yourself, and do what you know is right."

Pushing back his empty cereal bowl, Dad Miller reached for a Bible from the stack nearby. "I'll read a few verses from Exodus, for us to think about," he said. Carefully, he turned the thin pages until he found the place he wanted and read aloud.

'Thou shalt not raise a false report: put not thine hand with the wicked to be an unrighteous witness. Thou shalt not follow a multitude to do evil; neither shalt thou speak in a cause to decline after many to wrest judgement:'

"There are three phrases which talk about what we were discussing," he read on. "Put not thine hand with the wicked,' and 'Thou shalt not follow a multitude to do evil,' and 'Neither shalt thou decline after many to wrest judgement.' Children, there will be many times in your life when you will need to choose whether to follow a multitude to do evil, or do right and stand alone. It's good to remind ourselves often that we don't *have* to do everything others are doing! It's good to practice making our own choices, rather than following after 'in-things.'"

Dad closed the Bible and stood up. "You'd better run and get ready now," he reminded. "The school van will soon be here!"

When the children reached school, they were in for a surprise. Two of the school board members were there, and Brother Ken called an assembly of the whole school. "Brother Daniel will lead us in our devotions this morning," he announced, and sat down with his class.

The children waited expectantly. *What's going on?* Peter wondered. *Somebody must be in trouble or something!* He watched intently as Brother Daniel rose to face the students and teachers. "Good morning, boys and girls," the school board chairman began in his deep, mellow voice. "This morning I want to talk about making wise choices in life . . ."

Peter relaxed, listening to the calm voice as Brother Daniel read a Scripture, then went on to explain and talk about it. But suddenly, all the boys in the room jerked to attention as they heard him ask: "Now boys, I have a question for you. What is wrong with baseball cards, basketball cards and other sports cards?"

Breathlessly, Peter stared at Brother Daniel. He wanted to turn and sneak a glance at Henry, but he didn't dare. After a brief silence, the speaker smiled. "Well, boys, if you can't tell me, I will tell you," he said, and he did. Brother Daniel said many of the same things Mama had just told Peter that morning, and by the time he had finished Peter was glad, *very* glad, that there were no sports cards in *his* pocket.

"Boys, I was sorry to learn that there are some of you who have cards like these and have brought them to school," Brother Daniel said sadly. "After assembly, I want these boys to come to the principal's office: Henry, Andy, George, Frank, and Mervin. If there are any more of you who have disobeyed our school rule and brought sports cards, I expect you to be honest about it and come to the office too."

Whew! Peter sighed inwardly as he walked back to his classroom after prayer. *Am I ever glad I didn't get involved with* that *"in-thing"!*

And maybe his lingering memory of this good feeling helped Peter with what happened later that same afternoon. Brother Ken had released his students for their last recess of the day, but was staying in the classroom himself to help two girls who were having trouble in math.

"What shall we play? Joshua asked as the group of upper-grade boys drifted across the school-yard together. "We don't have enough time to play a real game."

"I know something fun!" George exclaimed. He stopped walking, and the other boys gathered around him. "You know how Mervin gets seizures sometimes?" he chuckled.

"Gets *what?*" Andy wondered.

"You know. *Seizures*," George replied. "He jerks and twitches, and his eyes go like this;" George demonstrated. "My family was at his place last night, and I saw him do it. It was weird!" He paused for breath. "Now, here's what let's do. Mervin didn't come outside yet; let's get ready, and when he comes out, let's all act like we're having seizures! See if he can guess what we're doing."

"Aw, that wouldn't be nice," Joshua said half-heartedly.

"Come on, don't act like a *girl*," George taunted. "Mervin's a big boy. We're not gonna make him cry!"

Nobody else spoke, and Peter looked around at the other boys. No matter what they did or said, he knew that making fun of Mervin's seizures was something *he* didn't want to do. *"Always think for yourself, and do what you know is right!"* Dad's words seemed to echo through his mind. *"You don't have to do what others do!"*

"I'm not going to do that," Peter spoke up quietly, but in a firm voice. "You don't know how bad Mervin would feel, even if he doesn't cry. "Let's go practice shooting a few baskets instead." Then, without waiting to see whether the others would follow, Peter turned and marched up the hill to the basketball court.

Behind him, Peter heard the sound of footsteps crunching in gravel. "Good for you, Pete!" Joshua muttered as he hurried past. Then came Andy, Henry and the others — even George!

Peter's heart was light as he broke into a run. Instead of being a follower, he had been a leader! *I'm so glad I stood up for what was right,* Peter thought. *Mocking Mervin would've been a very bad "in-thing"!*

18

Families
Jeremiah 35:5-10, 18, 19

"What shall we do with our extra recess time?" Frank asked Timmy as the fourth-graders came bursting out into the warm sunshine.

"Extra recess!" Philip cheered, following right at Timmy's heels. "Let's go up on the ballfield and practice hitting balls *way* back into the woods!"

"Let's wrestle instead," Darwin suggested. "I'm tired of playing ball." "Yeah! Let's wrestle!" Eugene agreed.

Timmy felt a sudden tightness inside. "No, let's not wrestle," he said quickly. "I . . . I'd rather do something else."

"You don't want to wrestle?" Darwin asked, in a tone of great disbelief.

"He's not allowed to wrestle at school," Frank said helpfully. "His family has a rule."

"But . . . but *why?*" Darwin persisted, staring at Timmy as if Timmy were a strange kind of animal he had never seen before.

Timmy was getting irritated. "Okay, I'm gonna ask *you* a question too," he said belligerently. "Why do you have to wear long-sleeved shirts, even when it's hot?"

Now it was Darwin's turn to look uncomfortable. "That's my parents' rule," he explained. "They say it's more modest."

"See, different parents have different rules," Philip said calmly. "So let's wrestle for a few minutes, just the four of us, and then we'll all go up to the ball field. The winners in wrestling will get to be first at bat!"

Frank, Eugene, and Darwin agreed with enthusiasm, and Timmy was silent. Turning away from his friends as they rolled and struggled happily in the green grass, he watched the first and second graders play dodge ball instead. His little sister Laura kicked the ball with all her might, then ran to first base. Timmy laughed as he watched.

Suddenly, though, he heard two little second-grade girls talking, and their words made him think about his own problem once more. "You mean you aren't allowed to eat any candy even if someone gives it to you? Your parents must be really strict!" Mary was saying to Rhoda.

"I guess so," Rhoda replied with a smile. "But

they aren't so particular as Dorcas' parents. *She's* not allowed to go barefoot until almost the middle of the summer, and she mustn't *ever* climb trees. I guess they are scared she'll fall and break her bones."

"And, did you know Paul and Sarah aren't allowed to read any books about animals that talk to each other, not even *Peter Rabbit?*" Mary told her friend. The two little girls giggled.

Parents, Timmy brooded as he walked slowly toward the ball diamond. *Why do they have to have different ideas and things like that? Life would be so much easier if everyone had exactly the same rules!* Kicking at a grass clump, he pounded his bat on the base and waited for his friends to join him. *I don't like to be different from my friends,* he muttered inwardly.

As teachers often do, Sister Joy observed more than the fourth-grade boys thought. When she led the devotional lesson the next morning, the teacher directed her class to the thirty-fifth chapter of Jeremiah.

"Children," she began, "have you ever felt like your parents were being unfair when they made rules that are different from the rules in your friends' families? I won't ask you to answer that question. But I'm sure you have all learned by now that different families have different rules. I'm going to read a story from the Bible, about a family who had different rules than the other families around them. Jeremiah thirty-five, starting at verse five;" Sister Joy said, and read aloud in her clear soft voice:

'And I set before the sons of the house of the Rechabites pots full of wine, and cups, and I said unto them, Drink ye wine. But they said, We will drink no wine: for Jonadab the son of Rechab our father commanded us, saying, Ye shall drink no wine, neither ye, nor your sons for ever: Neither shall ye build house, nor sow seed, nor plant vineyard, nor have any: but all your days ye shall dwell in tents; that ye may live many days in the land where ye be strangers. Thus have we obeyed the voice of Jonadab the son of Rechab our father in all that he hath charged us, to drink no wine all our days, we, our wives, our sons, nor our daughters; Nor to build houses for us to dwell in: neither have we vineyard, nor field, nor seed: But we have dwelt in tents, and have obeyed, and done according to all that Jonadab our father commanded us . . . And Jeremiah said unto the house of the Rechabites, Thus saith the Lord of hosts, the God of Israel. Because you have obeyed the commandment of Jonadab your father, and kept all his precepts, and done according to all that he hath commanded you: Therefore thus saith the Lord of Hosts, the God of Israel.

Jonadab the son of Rechab shall not want a man to stand before me forever.'

"In this Bible story, Jonadab was the father of a family who were called the 'Rechabites'," Sister Joy explained to her students. "Jonadab had some special rules for his family. They were not allowed to drink any wine, and he also didn't want them to build houses or plant gardens. Living in houses and planting gardens are not sinful, but Jonadab saw a spiritual value in doing without those things. He may have believed that if his children lived in tents, being herdsmen instead of settled farmers, they would remember that they were 'strangers' in the land. Jonadab wanted his family to remember that they were *God's* people, and heaven was their real home!

"Perhaps Jonadab's children sometimes wished that their father wouldn't have those 'strange' convictions. Maybe they wished they could just live like their friends did! But the Bible says that the children of Jonadab obeyed their father's rules, even after they were grown up. The Rechabites 'kept all the precepts' of Jonadab, their father, and God blessed them for it. God said that because of their obedience, the children of Jonadab would keep the faith. They would always have descendants who would worship God, for ever!"

Sister Joy paused, and smiled at her class. "Each of you has godly parents, too, who make rules and limits for you," she said. "They make rules for you because they love and care about you; to keep you safe and well, and to guard the purity of your minds and hearts. The rules and standards your parents set may be different from other families' rules. Every family has different ways of doing things, and that is all right.

"Sometimes you may be tempted to wish you could trade your family for someone else's family. But, did you know that God chose your family for you? *God* sets people in families, and He has chosen just the right family for each one of you. None of your parents are perfect people, but they love you and set standards because they care.

"There are two important things I want you to remember, boys and girls," Sister Joy went on. "Can you think of what the first one might be?"

Timmy raised his hand. "Always be obedient to your own parents' rules," he said quietly.

"That is right!" the teacher smiled in approval. "And here's the second important thing: *never* make fun of other families' convictions, and their ways of doing things, even though they are not the same as yours."

Looking across the aisle Timmy saw Darwin looking back at him. *We want to be like the Rechabites!* their eyes seemed to say, as the two friends smiled at each other.

19

Flowers for Sister Margie
Proverbs 12:25

Sister Margie was discouraged and sad. The world outdoors was gray and misty with a spring rain, and her heart felt gloomy too. *I wonder if God really wants me to be a teacher?* she thought, staring through her classroom window at the cloudy sky. *Some of my pupils were so naughty yesterday. I must not be doing a very good job! Maybe I'm not wise enough to be a teacher . . .*

Turning from the window, Sister Margie walked to her desk. It was after eight o'clock, and soon the boys and girls would be coming to school. *I must get ready for the day,* she told herself. *I must prepare the lessons, and be ready to smile at the children when they come in, even though I don't feel like smiling.*

Sister Margie bowed her head in prayer. "Lord, help me," she whispered. "I need your strength to face the day. Give me courage and wisdom, if you really want me to be a teacher." Then, feeling a little better, she opened her lesson-planning book.

The clock on the wall ticked away the minutes, one by one. Soon one van-load of children arrived, and then another. Happy voices rang through the halls, along with the sound of many young footsteps.

"Good morning, Sister Margie!" called one child after another, as they hung up jackets and plopped lunch boxes onto the shelves.

"Good morning, Paul," Sister Margie answered. "Good morning, Sarah. Good morning, Eric and Rachel!"

At five minutes till nine, a buzzer rang in the hallway. It was the signal for everyone to get one more drink, hurry to their classrooms and take their seats. At nine o'clock, each teacher would ring another bell on his or her desk. Any child who was not seated by then would be tardy! Sister Margie glanced around her room, and counted the pupils. *Everyone is here, except for Laura Miller,* she thought. *Where can Laura be? Oh, here she comes.*

"Hurry, Laura," the teacher said. I'm just about to ring the bell, so take your seat."

"Good morning, Sister Margie!" Laura replied cheerfully, walking over to her desk. Suddenly the little girl stopped short. "I forgot something!" she gasped. Turning around, she dashed from the room.

"Why, Laura!" Sister Margie was startled, and all the other children stared. What would the teacher do now? Wide-eyed, they waited to see what would happen.

In just a moment, Laura reappeared at the classroom door. Her face was glowing with excitement, and her hands were behind her back as if she were hiding something.

"Laura," Sister Margie began sternly, "what are you doing?"

"I have something for you, and I left it out on the hallway shelf!" Laura exclaimed, beaming with joy. Her hands came out from behind her back, and she held out a small white styrofoam cup full of purple violets.

"Here, these are for you," she told Sister Margie, with shining eyes. "God told me to bring you some flowers this morning! So I went out and picked these violets before breakfast, even though it was raining. Do you like them?"

The stern look on the teacher's face dissolved into surprise. "Why, yes, Laura. How pretty! Thank you," Sister Margie said, taking the cup of violets. She put one arm around Laura's shoulders in a little hug.

"I just knew God wanted me to give you some flowers this morning, 'cause you're such a wonderful teacher," Laura smiled happily as she turned back to her seat.

Tears came to Sister Margie's eyes, and she had to reach for a tissue to blow her nose. Then she rang the tardy bell, a couple of minutes later than usual, and began with morning worship time. But her whole day was changed! Not just by that pretty little cup of violets on her desk, but by Laura's words. *"God wanted me to bring you flowers . . . you're such a wonderful teacher."* Those words rang again and again through the teacher's mind. *God loves me!* her heart sang. *Just when I needed it, He sent me this encouragement through a first-grader!*

And Sister Margie remembered a verse from the Book of Proverbs: "Heaviness in the heart of man maketh it stoop; but a good word maketh it glad." (Proverbs 12:25) *My heart was stooped with heaviness, but little Laura's good word made it glad,* the teacher thought. For the rest of her life, whenever she read that verse, she would always think of violets . . . and a little girl who had obeyed God's prompting.

20

One More Ball
Mark 1:17, 18

"First!" shouted Henry, breaking into a run as soon as he was through the door. "Second!" Mervin cried as he ran after Henry, with his long legs pumping and a bat swinging from his right hand.

"I'm third!" Peter exclaimed, hurrying to catch up with the others flocking toward the ball-field. "This bat is going to hit a line drive today!"

"Hurry, let's hit a few practice balls before the teacher gets here," Joshua called. "I'm going out on the field to catch them!" Andy and George joined Joshua, pulling on their gloves and scattering out on the grassy field.

"What a nice day to play ball!" Peter told Mervin as they waited for their turn to bat. "It's not too hot, but the sun is shining. And listen to those birds!"

"You're not hearing the birds. Those are the *girls* you hear," Mervin quipped with a grin. "See, there they come, and Brother Ken too."

"Aww," Peter groaned in mock disappointment. "Now we will have to choose sides, and let the girls play too! Hurry and hit, Mervin, so I can have my turn yet."

The ball came flying back from the outfield, and Mervin picked it up. Tossing it lightly into the air above his right shoulder, he swung back his bat. *Crack!* There was a solid, crisp sound as he scored a perfect hit.

"Yay! that was a good one," Peter said admiring, watching the boys out in the field as they scrambled after the faraway ball. "You could've had a home run with that one, Mervin, if we were really playing."

Just then Brother Ken and the girls reached the edge of the ball field. "Okay, fellows," the teacher called, waving his arm toward the boys in a wide, beckoning gesture. "Come back in, and let's choose sides for a game!"

"Oh, no!" Peter moaned. "I didn't get my turn to hit yet!" He waved wildly to the boys who were still in the outfield. "Gimme the ball! Quickly! "

Joshua drew back his arm and sent the ball in a nice, easy curve, right into Peter's waiting hands. *I'll be quick*, Peter thought, determined to take his turn before he obeyed the teacher's order. *Just one more ball!*

In one swift, smooth motion, Peter bounced the ball into the air and swung. *Thwack!* His bat connected solidly, sending the ball straight out in a streaking blur of speed. The dreadful thing happened so quickly that Peter had no time to shout a warning. One instant he was seeing the whizzing ball, and his friend Joshua walking in toward second base. Joshua's eyes widened in sudden surprise as, too late, he noticed the ball. The next instant there was a sickening thud as the ball struck Joshua's cheekbone, right below his eye. The impact threw Joshua's whole body backward, his arms and legs flopping like a rag doll's as he fell to the ground.

One of the girls screamed, and Peter somehow found himself moving forward. Brother Ken was the first to reach his fallen pupil, with Peter and the other boys not far behind. As they approached, Joshua's eyes fluttered open and rolled sickeningly. *"He-e-elp me.* Somebody *help* me!" he moaned in a strange, feeble voice.

"Stand back, boys," Brother Ken said tensely as he knelt beside Joshua with his fingers on one limp wrist feeling for the pulse.

After a long moment, which seemed much longer to the anxious watchers, Joshua's consciousness returned and his eyes opened normally. "What ... happened?" he wondered, looking around at the circle of faces bending over him. The right side of his face, where the ball had hit him, was puffing up like a balloon.

"The ball hit you," Brother Ken replied. "Are you all right?"

"Yeah, I guess so," Joshua said bravely. He sat up slowly, looking embarrassed by all the attention. "It didn't hit my eye, and my teeth are all still there, and my nose isn't bleeding."

Brother Ken helped the injured boy to his feet. "Mary Lou, run down to the kitchen and bring a tea-towel full of ice cubes," he directed one of the older girls. "Joshua, we'll have you sit quietly over here in the shade and rest until this recess is over. Keep putting this ice on your bump, and tell me if you start feeling sick to your stomach."

Peter did not enjoy the ball game that noon. Every time he looked at poor Joshua, sitting in the shade with the ice-pack clasped against his swollen face, Peter felt uncomfortable and guilty. *It was really my fault,* he thought miserably. *If only I hadn't hit that one last ball! I didn't obey Brother Ken right away, and now look what happened . . .*

"Boys and girls," Brother Ken began when the class was seated at their desks once more, "we must thank the Lord that Joshua does not seem to be seriously injured. And I think we can all learn a lesson from this experience, too."

He paused, and Peter felt his face grow hot. Was everyone staring at *him*? He kept his eyes on his desktop. "In the gospel of Mark," the teacher went on, we often see the word 'straightway'. When Jesus called Simon Peter and Andrew, for example, they *straightway* forsook their nets and followed Him. What do you think this word means?"

"Right now, or immediately," one of the girls volunteered.

"Yes, that is right," Brother Ken replied. "The right kind of obedience is *prompt* obedience. When we are called, we must obey right away. My father used to say, *'Delayed obedience is disobedience!'* And today you saw a good example of trouble which could have been avoided by prompt obedience. After this, I hope you will all be more careful to obey promptly. When you are called, obey *straightway!* Don't read one more chapter . . . or grab one more cookie . . . or hit one more ball."

Turning in his Bible to the book of Mark, Brother Ken found the verses he wanted and read aloud:

"'And Jesus said unto them, come ye after me, and I will make you to become fishers of men. And straightway they forsook their nets, and followed him.' Mark 1:17 and 18."

Peter could only nod his head in agreement. *Straightway,* he thought. *After this I want to obey straightway!*

21

The Cough Drop
Proverbs 12:22

"I'm all finished with my work, Sister Margie. What shall I do now?" Jason wondered.

The teacher smiled at her eager first-grade boy. "I believe your desk needs to be cleaned out," she suggested. "You have too many extra papers inside. Give it a good spring cleaning, and organize things neatly."

Jason grinned happily. Raising the lid of his desk, he began pushing the books and papers around. But the desk lid would not stay up as it was supposed to, and Jason began to find organizing a difficult job with only one hand. Sister Margie soon noticed his problem.

"Jason," she spoke quietly from the other side of the room where she was helping the second-graders, "you may get a ruler from my top desk drawer and use it to prop up your lid."

Out of the corner of her eye, the teacher observed Jason as he hurried to obey. In a moment, he was walking back to his desk with Sister Margie's stout wooden ruler in his hand. But what was wrong with Jason now? His teacher's alert eye could see the telltale signs of a guilty conscience. Jason's head was up, but his eyes were furtive. His shoulders were stiff, *too* stiff. He was trying to pretend that nothing was wrong, but Sister Margie could read the signs all too well!

Still holding the second grade math book, Sister Margie slowly made her way across the room until she stood by Jason's desk. "Jason, what do you have in your mouth?" she asked softly.

"A cough drop," Jason mumbled back, as he crumpled several papers into a wad.

"Where did you get it?" the teacher wondered, thinking of the bag of cough drops she kept in her desk drawer to give to children who needed them.

"I found it in my desk," Jason replied quickly, but his eyes still could not look at his teacher.

"Jason, I think you had better put your head down on your desk and think about this," Sister Margie told him in a low voice. "What do you think Jesus would want you to tell me?"

Tears sprang into the little boy's eyes. Quickly he closed his desk, and laid his head on his folded arms; then just as quickly he raised his head again. "Teacher, I took it out of your drawer," he said, choking with sobs. "The devil told me I should take it, 'cause you would never know. I'm sorry I told a lie!"

Sister Margie knelt in the aisle and put her arm around the first-grader. "I'm glad you told me the truth now, Jason," she told him. "Lying is an abomination to the Lord, which means God hates lying very much. He wants us to always speak the truth."

Sister Margie reached for a wad of crumpled paper from Jason's desk. "Here, Jason, you may get rid of that cough drop," she said. "Put it into this paper, and take it to the wastebasket. Then, at recess time, I will give you a Bible verse to copy and learn by heart."

Sister Margie handed Jason a clean sheet of tablet paper. Across the top she had printed this verse: "Lying lips are abomination to the Lord: but they that deal truly are His delight." Proverbs 12:22.

"Jason, I want you to copy this verse ten times on the paper," she told the first grader. "And each time you write the verse, say it to yourself. You want to memorize this verse and hide it in your heart, to help you the next time Satan tempts you to tell a lie. Now, let's read the verse together, to make sure you know all the words:

"'Lying lips are abomination to the Lord: but they that deal truly are His delight.' Proverbs 12:22," Jason and his teacher recited together.

22

School Days in Belize
Isaiah 52:7

"*When* will the teachers be here?" Laura wondered aloud for the fourth time, looking up from the napkins she was folding for the dinner table.

"Mom invited them for supper at six-thirty," Sharon reminded her little sister. She placed a bouquet of fresh wildflowers in the center of the table, and stood back to admire their effect.

"I'm glad we're finally having the teachers over," said Peter as he snitched a ripe olive from the relish tray. "This school year will soon be finished, and we didn't have our turn yet."

"Peter Miller, you leave that relish tray alone!" Sharon scolded. "We want everything to look nice for the teachers."

"Here comes Brother Ken!" Timmy exclaimed as he passed the window. "And here come the others right behind him!"

Brother Ken was soon standing at the Millers' front door with his wife and four small daughters, followed by Sister Margie and Sister Joy. "Come in!" "Welcome!" the Millers greeted them gladly.

Mama took their supper of home made pizza out of the oven, and the group was soon enjoying it together. With so many teachers present, the conversation was often about school.

"How many years have you been teaching, Brother Ken?" Dad wondered as Mama served the dessert and poured cups of tea.

"This year is my seventeenth year," Peter and Sharon's teacher replied. "I've been here at Sunnyside School for ten years, and before that I taught for seven years in Belize."

"Oh, tell us some stories about Belize!" Timmy spoke up. "Sister Brenda, my first grade teacher, is there now."

"Well, school days in Belize are quite different from school days here," Brother Ken began. "The weather in Belize is nearly always very hot, so they don't need big, sturdy school buildings like we have here. Nice books and equipment are not so plentiful there, either."

"Did the children there play games at recess, and have programs too, like us?" Laura asked, thinking of the poem she was memorizing for poetry day.

Brother Ken laughed. "I remember a school

program once, which didn't go too well," he answered. "My students had done a good job of learning songs and memorizing poems and passages of Scripture to recite. But when their big evening came, the weather was hotter than usual. Every bench in that little wooden church building was packed with parents, friends and neighbors, and more people were standing at the back. Many of my students that year were shy, timid children, and perhaps the sight of all those people watching, together with the heat, was too much for them. The children were standing on the platform in the front of the room, doing their best to sing, with sweat trickling down their faces. Suddenly one boy turned ashy pale, and slumped to the floor, unconscious. He had fainted! Two men came forward and carried him outdoors to revive him. I encouraged the other children to keep on with their presentation, and they tried bravely. But it wasn't long before a second child fainted, and then another! One by one, half my class keeled over where they stood. Nobody suffered any lasting damage, but it sure spoiled our program!"

"I remember another program in Belize," said Sister Joy, "but this story had a better ending. I had a class of nine first-graders that year. They had memorized the old story of how Jesus came to visit Martin, the shoemaker, and each one had his part to say. But several of the boys had colds in the days before the program, and one of them lost his voice completely! 'What shall we do, children?' I asked my class the morning of the program. 'Myron can't make a sound except a whisper. Shall we let someone else try to learn his part and say it for him?'

"'Let's pray, Teacher,' one little black boy suggested. 'Yes, God could make Myron better!' someone agreed.

"We had no loudspeaker system in that church building, so the children's voices needed to be loud and clear. I must confess that I was doubtful! God *could* heal Myron's voice, but *would* He? My children wanted to pray, though, so we prayed. When evening came, Myron was still hoarse. So we had another prayer meeting just before the program . . . and when the time came for Myron to say his part, his voice was triumphantly strong and loud! Later, I reminded the boys to thank God for answering our prayer.

"'Teacher, I *knew* God would do it,' little Darrel told me. 'So, I thanked Him right away!'"

"You taught school in Belize too, didn't you?" asked Sharon. "Did you have a lot of adventures when God answered prayer?"

"Yes, there were many," Sister Joy replied reverently. "My students at the mission school were mostly black children, whose parents did not have much knowledge of the Scripture. But those little children's faith often surprised me! Did I ever tell you children about the 'steering wheel with arthritis'?"

"No! you never did," said Timmy quickly. "Tell the story now!"

Sister Joy chuckled softly. "The mission car was pretty old," she began, "and its power steering was going bad. I had to work really hard to turn the steering wheel, because I'm not very big. One Sunday morning I used the car to pick up a load of little village girls and bring them to church. After church, the little girls climbed into the car with me again. I started the engine, and got ready to use all my muscle to turn out of the church yard. To my amazement, the steering wheel turned very easily! I looked very surprised, and the girls giggled.

"'Miss Joy, does it turn easier now?' asked a child named Karina.

"'Yes, it does! I'm so glad!' I told her.

"'Well, Miss Joy, I saw how hard you had to work to turn it this morning,' said Karina. 'So I asked God to fix the steering wheel's arthritis while we were in church, and He fixed it!'"

"You were a mission teacher too before you were married, weren't you?" Brother Ken asked Mrs. Miller.

"Yes, I taught in Belize and Costa Rica," Mama answered.

"Aren't there a lot of dangerous bugs and snakes in those countries?" Sister Margie wondered with a little shiver.

"Oh, yes, but you get used to it," Mama laughed. "I learned to keep a broom handy in my classroom for killing scorpions, so they wouldn't sting the children in my care. And I managed to smile politely when one of my third-graders brought his huge, hairy black tarantula spider to school. There was one time I *did* scream, though, and that was when I was walking alone and stepped right on a poisonous snake. I don't know which was more frightened, me or the snake! But we both moved pretty quickly."

"God watches over His missionaries," Dad Miller observed. "All those who leave their homes and families for the sake of the Gospel will find great blessings, in this life *and* the next. Whenever I think of missionaries, I think of this verse from Isaiah:

"'How beautiful upon the mountains are the feet of him that bringeth good tidings, that publisheth peace; that bringeth good tidings of good, that publisheth salvation; that saith unto Zion, thy God reigneth!'"

"It is a beautiful thing to bring good tidings of peace to the world, and missionaries are special people! I'm glad we have so many of you here this evening," Dad said.

How beautiful upon the mountains . . . are the missionaries! Sharon thought, and her eyes were bright with hopes and dreams for the future. *If the Lord calls me, how I would love to be a missionary teacher too!*

23

Under His Wings

Psalm 91

One sunny afternoon in spring, Mama came to pick up the Miller children at school. "Are we going to town?" Peter wondered, climbing into the front seat of the station wagon. "Hi, there, Beffy!" he greeted his chubby little sister.

"BEE-ter!" Beth crowed happily in reply, trying to climb out of her car seat.

"No, stay sitting, Beth," Mama replied hastily. "And yes, I am planning to do a little shopping," she answered Peter as the other three children got into the car.

"Where will we go first, Mom?" Sharon asked, looking out the window at the passing scenery.

"I need to stop at McArtor's Corner Grocery," Mama replied. After carefully looking both ways, she guided the car across the busy highway and

148

turned into the store's tiny parking lot.

"This will only take me a minute," Mama announced briskly. "You children can all wait in the car. Peter, keep Beth happy!" and with a smile, she was gone.

"Mama!" Beth whimpered.

"Now, Beffy, Mama will be right back," Peter comforted. "Look, do you want to drivey-drivey?" Unfastening his little sister's carseat, he helped Beth stand on the driver's seat and hold the steering wheel. "Now Beth can drive the car, just like Mama and Daddy," he told her. "Drivey-drivey!" Beth squealed in triumph.

Then the shiny keys dangling in the ignition caught her eye. "This!" Beth said, reaching for the keys.

"Oh, no! You mustn't touch the keys. That's no-no," Peter told her hastily. "You might start the car. Leave the keys alone!" Beth looked wide-eyed at her brother.

"Here, drivey-drivey," Peter repeated. "Just hold the big wheel, and you can drive. You mustn't touch the keys or the gear stick, though."

Then it happened. Peter's attention was drawn to his window, away from the little girl, and in that instant Beth grasped the gear lever. She leaned on the lever, trying to reach those tempting keys. With a jerk, the car slipped into reverse. Tires crunching on the gravel, the Millers' station wagon began slowly rolling backwards down the slope.

149

"What's happening?" Sharon cried out in alarm from the back seat. "Peter, stop her! We'll roll right onto the highway!"

Whirling around, Peter seized the gearshift and tried to push it back into *Park*. But since the wheels were rolling, he couldn't get it in. "I can't get it!" Peter gasped in frustration as the car continued to roll. Setting his teeth, he pushed with all his might.

Bonk! BOOONNK! a horn blared loudly, and the Miller children looked back in horror to see a huge semitrailer truck barreling down the highway toward them.

"If we keep rolling back, he'll hit us!" Sharon moaned.

Instantly, Peter knew what he had to do. Grabbing little Beth, he yanked her over and down to the floor between his feet. Then he was up, scrambling over the carseat which blocked his way, and sliding into the driver's seat in a blur of arms and legs. He stomped on the brake, and the station wagon finally came to a grinding halt on the very edge of the highway. Reaching for the keys in the ignition, he turned the car key forward and stepped on the gas pedal. The engine started, and Peter hit the gearshift into *Drive*. The station wagon lurched forward, just as a mighty rumble and the hissing of air brakes behind told the Millers that the semi-truck had safely passed them by!

Carefully, Peter drove the car the rest of the

way back up to the grocery store entrance. As he was doing so, Mama came through the door and stared in surprise at the scene before her. *"Why is Peter driving the car?"* she gasped, as she moved quickly to join her family.

"Thank the Lord you are safe!" Mama said when her trembling children told their story. She cuddled the frightened, crying baby Beth. "We'd better not let her play in the drivers' seat again," Mama concluded. "I've heard of little children wrecking cars that way."

When Dad Miller heard what had happened, he also gave thanks to God. "Let's read Psalm 91 tonight for our devotional meditation," he said. "It tells us about God's care and protection. There are so many times when He keeps us safe under His wings!

"'He that dwelleth in the secret place of the most High shall abide under the shadow of the Almighty,' Dad read aloud. 'I will say of the LORD, He is my refuge and my fortress: my God; in him will I trust. Surely he shall deliver thee . . . He shall cover thee with his feathers, and under his wings shalt thou trust . . . thou shalt not be afraid . . . He shall give His angels charge over thee, to keep thee in all thy ways . . .'"

The familiar words of the Psalm had new meaning for Peter that evening. *I'm so glad God helped me know what to do, and to do it quickly,* he thought. *I'm so glad we were under His wings!*

24

Report Card Day
I Samuel 7:7-12

"School's OUT!" Peter shouted gleefully as he burst through the double doors into the parking lot. Tossing his empty lunchbox high into the air, he ran a few hasty steps forward to catch it as it came down.

Timmy followed his older brother more soberly, his arms full of books and papers, but his eyes shone with excitement too. *The first day of school was exciting, but today is better yet!* he thought. *School is out for the summer! Now I can stay home and go swimming . . . and fishing . . . and set traps for groundhogs that get in the garden . . .*

A group of little girls were next to come through the schoolhouse doors, all chattering and giggling at once. "Do you have your report card, Laura?" Sarah Beth reminded.

"Yes I do," Laura answered, holding up the slim brown envelope. Her eyes sparkled as she thought of the good news it contained.

Sharon's feelings were mixed as she came through the door on this last, special day. Her years at Sunnyside Christian School were ended now. *Maybe I will come back as a teacher, but never as a pupil!* Sharon thought, and her joy in growing up struggled briefly with the pain of loosing something familiar and precious. The Miller family's church school did not continue through all the high-school grades, so Sharon and her classmates would not be back next year.

"Good-bye!" "Good-bye!" "See you at church!" children called to their friends as they separated and ran to the waiting cars and vans.

Mama was there with the Millers' old station wagon, and Laura bounded over to meet her. "Mama, look at my report card!" she squealed happily as she climbed into the car. Dropping her armload of used workbooks and papers, she handed the report card envelope to her mother.

"Well, well," Mama said, looking down at her eager daughter. "Do you mean you didn't 'flunk' after all?"

"No, of course I didn't. And my report card has nothing but straight 'A's, all year!" Laura beamed.

Peter and Timmy were getting into the car, and Sharon slid into the front seat last of all. Carefully she put the envelope containing her report card into a safe place, then turned to take one last look at Sunnyside School as the car began to move . . .

That evening when the Miller family gathered for their devotions, Dad smiled as he looked around at the circle of his four scholars.

"Well, children, another school year is over," he said. "That reminds me of a verse in the Bible . . . 'Hitherto hath the Lord helped us'! God has helped each of you through the school year, and we must give thanks to Him."

"'Hitherto hath the Lord helped us!' Where is that verse, Dad?" Timmy wondered.

"It is found in the seventh chapter of First Samuel," Dad explained. "The children of Israel had gathered to fast and pray before the Lord, and when the Philistines heard about this revival meeting, they decided to come with their armies and attack them. The Israelites were very frightened when they saw their enemies approaching! 'Cry unto the Lord for us, that He will save us out of the hands of the Philistines!' they said to one another. And the Bible says that the Lord heard them, and 'thundered with a great thunder' upon the Philistines."

"Does that mean the Philistines' armies were struck by lightning?" asked Peter.

"It might mean that," Dad replied. "Or at least the thunder frightened the Philistines so badly that they panicked. 'So, the Philistines were discomfited and frightened, and the men of Israel pursued them and smote them.' After their mighty victory, the prophet Samuel set up a great stone in memory of that day. He called the stone *Ebenezer,* meaning, 'Hitherto hath the Lord helped us.'"

"Well, children, can you think of some special ways that the Lord helped you during this school year?" Mama asked, looking from one face to another.

"I was *so* scared the first day of school. I thought I was going to flunk," Laura remembered, giggling. "But then I prayed, and God helped me not to be afraid. And I really *didn't* flunk, either!" she finished, thinking of that report card full of 'A's.

"I guess God helped me lots of times," Timmy mused. "Like the time my friends wanted to play a shooting game but I knew we shouldn't, and I asked them *'What would Jesus do?'* The Lord helped me to be brave that day."

"God helped me to know what to do the time when Beth made the car roll! And He helped me to get better grades in math and English," Peter said with satisfaction. "In the beginning of the year, Brother Ken kept saying that I wasn't trying hard enough. So I asked God to help me, and Dad prayed about it too, and then I *wanted* to work harder. So now my report card shows better grades than it used to."

"I can't *find* my report card," Sharon spoke up, her face troubled. "And I never even had a chance to open it! I've looked all through my books and papers, and on the floor in the car, and behind the seat, but it just doesn't seem to be anywhere. I can't think what I might have done with it."

"Don't forget to pray about it," Dad suggested. "Ask the Lord to help you find your report card, and surely it will turn up!"

When the family knelt to pray, Sharon's mind went to the missing report card. *"Lord, I need my report card,"* she spoke silently. *"I can't think where it is, but You know where it is! Please help me find it again, according to Your will."*

And even as Sharon prayed, a picture seemed to spring into her mind. She saw herself getting into the car at school, with the report card on top the pile of books and papers. She had picked up the report card envelope and reached up to slide it between the sun-visor flap and the car ceiling, where it had stayed safely out of sight and out of her mind until now!

Yes! That's what I did with it, Sharon exclaimed inwardly. *Thank you, Lord!*

When the family's prayers were ended, Sharon jumped to her feet. "God reminded me where I put my report card, just as soon as I prayed," she told the others happily. "I'm going out to get it, right now."

Slipping her hand into the sun-visor, Sharon grasped the missing envelope at last.

'Hitherto hath the Lord helped us,' she thought to herself as she ran back to the house to show her report card to her parents. *It's been a great year!*